"I saw
look

"You liked what you saw, Miss Roberts,"
Logan went on softly. "But you were
damned determined not to admit it."

Color flooded Talia's cheeks. "You
flatter yourself."

"Do I?" He laughed. Then he pulled her
into his arms with a speed that took her
breath away.

"No." Panic turned her voice
thready. "Don't—"

His mouth silenced her, his kiss gentling,
deepening. With a sob of desperation,
Talia pushed hard against his chest and
twisted free.

"Are you always this brave," she said, after
her heart had stopped racing, "or is it
because I'm a woman that you think you
can take what you want?"

He laughed. "If you mean do I always get
what I want, the answer is yes."

SANDRA MARTON says she's always believed in romance. She wrote her first love story when she was nine and fell in love at sixteen with the man who is her husband. Today they live on Long Island, midway between the glitter of Manhattan and the quiet beaches of the Atlantic. Sandra is delighted to be writing the kinds of stories she loves and even happier to find that her readers enjoy them, too.

Books by Sandra Marton

HARLEQUIN PRESENTS

Don't miss any of our special offers. Write to us at the following address for information on our newest releases.

Harlequin Reader Service
P.O. Box 1397, Buffalo, NY 14240
Canadian address: P.O. Box 603,
Fort Erie, Ont. L2A 5X3

SANDRA MARTON

consenting adults

Harlequin Books

TORONTO • NEW YORK • LONDON
AMSTERDAM • PARIS • SYDNEY • HAMBURG
STOCKHOLM • ATHENS • TOKYO • MILAN

For Barf
Doctor T agrees—there's no place like home

Harlequin Presents first edition July 1991
ISBN 0-373-11379-X

Original hardcover edition published in 1990
by Mills & Boon Limited

CONSENTING ADULTS

CHAPTER ONE

TALIA held the grey flannel suit against her as she stared into the mirror. Not bad, she thought, tilting her head critically. The suit, along with the matching kidskin pumps and the cream silk blouse still in her suitcase, was the perfect dress-for-success ensemble. She'd look calm and professional, an example of middle management at its respectable best.

Nobody would suspect that in reality she was a quaking bundle of nerves, ready to come unglued at the first touch.

She sighed as she hung the suit in the wardrobe. Her boss knew that she was a wreck, of course, but he wasn't here. John was back in the San Francisco office, which was where he'd called from minutes ago.

'Break a leg, kid,' he'd said cheerfully, and Talia had winced. Somehow, she'd have preferred a simple 'good luck' to the traditional actor's phrase. But John Diamond had pursued a fruitless stage career before he'd started Diamond Food Services, and he never tired of re-minding anyone who'd listen that his heart was still in the theatre. His expertise, however, was in catering—hotels, schools, and now lucrative corporate accounts.

Which was, Talia thought as she finished unpacking, the reason she was here, in a hotel on a wind-swept curve of northern California beach, about to take the first big step in her career. The thought turned her throat dry. She sank down on the edge of the bed and folded her hands in her lap.

You can do this, she thought, meeting her eyes in the mirror. John wouldn't have entrusted Miller

International's Executive Weekend to you if you weren't up to it.

Talia turned that over in her mind for a while. Of course she could do it. Two years working at a restaurant, four for a hotel chain, then three more at Diamond Food Services, working first in the kitchen, then in purchasing, finally in administration as John's assistant, had given her the practical experience needed to temper the time she'd spent gaining a degree in hotel and restaurant management. She knew her stuff. There was nothing immodest about admitting it.

She only wished she felt calmer. Talia, always practical, had planned her career with cool precision. The step up—the one she was about to take—had been one she'd expected in two years' time. That it had fallen into her lap so soon was as jarring as it was exciting. Sometimes she had a suspicion that that was part of the reason John had given it to her.

'This is liable to be a tough one, sweetheart,' he'd said when the letter from Miller International had first reached his desk. 'Their president says he wants us to set up a weekend retreat for upper-echelon execs; our choice of facility so long as it's somewhere very private— his words—along the coast.'

Talia had smiled. 'Private, hmm? What does his company do?'

Her boss had leaned back in his chair, crossed his arms behind his head, and grinned wickedly. 'It makes money. If they want a secluded spot, they can have one.' His grin had broadened. 'In the old days, that would have meant they were into primal scream therapy for the overpaid and underworked,' he'd said with the roguish aplomb of one who had survived the weirdness of California in the 1960s.

Talia had nodded. 'Right. Quiche and alfalfa sprouts. But surely that's not what they want today?'

'Not they, sweetheart. He. Mr Logan Miller. He's Miller International—has been for the past forty years—and what he wants, he gets, even if it turns out to be strange.' John had leaned forward and pushed the letter across the desk towards her. 'Suppose you telephone him and find out what he has in mind.'

The suggestion had surprised her. 'Me? But that's Harry's job.'

'Didn't I tell you? I've asked him to head up the new office in Seattle.' Her boss had winked. 'You get to do the dirty deed instead.'

Talia had tried to sound nonchalant, even though her heart was pounding. 'Are you offering me Harry's job?' she'd asked.

'Caught you by surprise, didn't I?' Laughter had glinted in John's eyes. 'You can't plan everything in life, Talia.' But you can try. The thought had come immediately, but she had suppressed it just as quickly. When she'd said nothing, John had looked at her. 'Don't you want it?'

'Of course I want it,' she'd said, forcing aside the images of brown rice casseroles and fertilised egg omelettes that had insisted on dancing through her mind.

She'd shaken hands on her promotion, then hurried back to her tiny office with the letter from Logan Miller clutched in her hand. Reading it had calmed her. Typed on heavy vellum, signed with a firm, masculine scrawl, it had detailed a Friday night through Sunday morning retreat planned for executives of the corporation's West Coast offices. When she'd got to the schedule and list of workshops that had been included, she had breathed a sigh of relief. The workshops were all business—Finance Strategies for Buyout Leverage had been one of the few comprehensive titles. Even the recreational activities had sounded wearing. The least strenuous was a dawn run along the beach.

Logan Miller couldn't be a day under sixty-five, but he'd planned a tough weekend. There'd be no brown rice or fertilised eggs for this lot, Talia had thought, and a phone call to Miller's Los Angeles office had confirmed it. Not that she'd spoken to Mr Miller; he was, his secretary had said, in Brazil on business. Mr Miller's food preferences? Lean meats. Fresh fish. Salads. Fresh vegetables.

Of course, Talia had thought, scribbling notes furiously, a man of Miller's age would be interested in a low-fat diet.

And yes, the secretary had said, the facility needed to be removed from the pressures of civilisation. Mr Miller wanted to ensure that his people had no distractions to keep them from the activities of the weekend. Was there anything else Miss Roberts needed?

'Yes,' Talia had said. 'When may I speak with Mr Miller?'

'He'll contact you if there's any need, Miss Roberts. But I'm sure you'll be able to handle things admirably.'

Talia had taken the polite hint. Logan Miller was not to be bothered with details. She'd set to work, making arrangements and sending copies of everything to his office. But the final decision about where to hold the weekend, had hardly seemed a detail. When she'd narrowed her choices to two, she'd sent Miller a letter asking for his recommendation. Both hotels were equally suitable, it was simply a matter of taste, et cetera, et cetera, et cetera.

She'd sat back to await his reply.

It had come by express mail. Logan Miller's note had been terse. It had said that he had no time to bother with such details, which was why he'd turned the job over to a catering corporation in the first place. And, if both hotels were equally suitable, why had he been asked to choose one over the other? He'd added that he doubted if either choice was appropriate anyway, and if that was the best she could manage, he could always take his business elsewhere. The note had ended with a handwritten, scrawled postscript. What of the Redwood Inn? it had asked. If memory served, it was perfect for the kind of weekend his organisation had planned.

Miller's response had at first upset Talia and then had infuriated her. Do the job yourself, he'd said, and then he'd proceeded to take it over. Coolly, Talia had sent off an answer, telling him he could, of course, choose the Redwood Inn. But the inn was closed for the season. Arrangements were possible, but would cost twice what her other suggestions would. There would be union fees, staffing fees...

His answering note had been a barely legible scrawl. 'Do it,' he'd written across the bottom of her letter.

And Talia had; she had planned everything, right down to the last detail, and it had cost a fortune, more than twice what she'd proposed. Her boss had turned pale when she'd shown him the final bill, but she'd shrugged and reminded him that Miller had approved the cost without comment.

In her heart, she'd thought that the increase was no more than Logan Miller deserved. But the vengeful thought was so unlike her that she'd kept it to herself. She prided herself on level-headed behaviour; that an old man she'd never met could anger her enough to bring out such an emotional side to her personality was embarrassing.

Now, hours before the cocktail party that would signal the start of the carefully planned weekend, she thought, grudgingly, that Miller had been right. The Redwood Inn, perched on a hill overlooking the Pacific, with the beach at its feet and a forest of giant redwoods at its back, was perfect.

She finished putting away the rest of her things, then glanced at her watch. Her staff would be well into their preparations by now. It was time to check and see how they were doing. They were all seasoned veterans, but it never hurt to check things yourself.

Talia stripped off the silk shirtwaist dress she'd travelled in. Kitchens were not only places of spills and stains, they were also invariably hot, especially in the dog-days of September. Shorts, a cotton-knit top and a pair of sandals would do. No one would see her except her staff, she thought, taking a quick glance into the mirror and smoothing back a strand of dark auburn hair.

Her pulse gave a nervous leap, and she made a face at herself. There was nothing more to worry about until the weekend really got under way. Still, she took a deep breath before she left her room.

The kitchen was a whirl of activity. Her people barely acknowledged her presence. Everyone was busy, going from the huge refrigerators to the stoves...

Talia frowned. No, not everyone. The back door was open, probably to catch any breeze that drifted by. A man lounged in the doorway, watching the flurry of proceedings with an impassive expression on his face. He was leaning on the frame, arms crossed against his chest, feet crossed at the ankles, looking like a casual spectator at a sporting match.

He turned towards her, their eyes met, and a lazy smile tilted at the corners of his mouth. For some reason it made her feel uncomfortable, and she looked away from him.

'Do we have enough shrimps?' she asked no one in particular. 'And what about oysters and clams?'

There were plenty of oysters and shrimps. And the clams had just been delivered. Did she want to check them herself? Minutes later, Talia had forgotten all about the man in the doorway. She was, instead, intent on tasting a Welsh rarebit that was simmering on the stove.

She hesitated, the spoon halfway to her mouth, as she felt a prickling along her skin. Slowly, almost reluctantly, she looked up. The stranger was watching her.

Even at a distance, there was no missing the intensity of his gaze.

Talia felt a slow flush rise along her skin. The shorts she was wearing were old and faded, the knit top loose and virtually shapeless. But she was suddenly aware of how skimpy an outfit it was.

His eyes moved over her, and she felt as if he were stripping the clothing from her body. The insolence of the man! And what was he doing in the kitchen of the Redwood Inn? There was no reason to see anyone but her staff in here right now. There'd be others in and out of the room tonight, when the extra servers that had been hired showed up. But that was hours away. And . . .

Of course. That was what he was—a temporary worker, hired to pass trays of hors-d'oeuvre and wait table this evening. There'd been no problem arranging for half a dozen such people: California beach communities tended to collect drifters who followed the sun and the surf, and drifters took work wherever they could.

The man in the doorway had that look, Talia thought, her glance moving dismissively over him. He was tall, leanly muscled, wearing ragged-edged cut-off denims and a T-shirt inscribed with what seemed to be a college seal, so faded it was illegible. She could almost picture him with a surfboard under his arm, although he seemed to be in his late thirties. Well, this was California. She'd seen stranger things than over-age beach bums since she'd moved West.

The stranger was smiling under her scrutiny, a very private, intimate smile, and a coldness clamped down on Talia's heart. Did he really think that would work with her? Carefully, she put down the spoon and moved towards him. 'May I help you?'

His teeth flashed in a quick grin. 'I don't know. What do you have in mind?'

He was good-looking, in an obvious kind of way, and he was probably used to doing rather well with women. Well, he was in for a surprise.

'Keep it up,' she said quietly, 'and you won't have to worry about tonight.'

His eyebrows rose in surprise. 'My, my,' he said teasingly, 'that's a pretty direct approach.'

'What I meant,' Talia said sharply, 'was that if you go on like this, you won't have a job to come to this evening.' He looked blank, and she sighed. 'You're here to work the cocktail party and dinner, aren't you?'

'Ah.' The smile came again. He stepped away from the wall and nodded. 'The Miller thing. I suppose you might say that, yes.'

A lock of auburn hair fell over Talia's forehead and she brushed it back impatiently. 'You're due here at seven. Until then, you're just in the way.' Her eyes moved over him again. 'I take it you can put your hands on black trousers? We'll provide the jacket and bow-tie.'

He laughed and put his hands on his hips. The movement made the muscles roll beneath his skin, and she thought, yes, definitely a surfer with that sun-bleached hair and taut body. Only someone who spent his time in constant activity could look so—so...

'And a white shirt,' she said, while a flush ran up under her skin.

He nodded. 'Yes, ma'am,' he said solemnly. 'Black trousers, white shirt. Anything else, Miss...?'

'And black shoes. Polished, of course.'

A grin tugged at his mouth. 'Of course. Miss—Miss...'

'Roberts.' Her voice was crisp. 'Talia Roberts. I'm in charge.'

The man stared at her for a minute, and then he took a step towards her. 'How nice to meet you,' he said, holding out his hand. 'And I'm——'

'I don't care in the least who you are,' she said coldly.

His smile dimmed a little. 'That's not very polite, Talia. When you deal with people, you might——'

Her chin rose. 'My name is Miss Roberts. And if I need advice, I'll certainly not ask for it from someone like you.'

The man's eyes narrowed. 'If I were you, Miss Roberts——'

'But you're not. And if you want to get paid tonight, you'd better learn to do as you're told.'

His smile turned to ice. 'Are you always this unpleasant to the people who work for you?'

No, she thought in surprise, she wasn't. Courtesy to staff was one of the things she prided herself on. Then why, she wondered, was she being so rude to him? The answer came quickly. Because he was impertinent. Because he had no business here. Because—because he made her uncomfortable and edgy and——

'Dammit to hell!'

The chef's voice roared across the kitchen as the Welsh rarebit boiled over. Talia took one look and grabbed for a towel. When she turned around again, the man had vanished.

She forget all about him as the afternoon passed. There were a dozen last-minute crises, none—thank goodness—that couldn't be handled. Finally, with only moments to spare, Talia hurried to her room to shower and change for the evening. When she was dressed, she looked into the mirror and smiled. She'd been right, the grey suit and silk blouse were perfect. She looked as cool and collected as ...

Talia jumped. For a second, her reflection had seemed to waver; she'd imagined she'd seen the stranger looking back at her, smiling his insolent smile.

She turned away sharply and picked up her bag. If the man showed up, which she doubted, she'd tell her people to keep a careful eye on him. He was more likely to try and skive off than work. He might even try to come on to the few women executives scattered in the group, and she didn't need that kind of headache. The cocktail party, and the dinner following, would bring enough problems of their own.

The hall was silent. The inn was three storeys high, and Logan Miller's people had all been housed on the first two levels. Talia had taken a room on the third floor, where she could monitor things without intruding on them.

Her heels clicked loudly as she walked down the corridor. The floating staircase loomed ahead, an impressive structure of redwood, stainless steel and glass. She paused at the top, her hand on the polished wood railing, and looked down. In a little while, all her months of planning and hard work would come together. And everything would be fine—she'd left nothing to chance.

'You're such a stickler for detail, Talia,' one of her assistants had said today, smiling. 'I bet it runs in the family.'

Wryly, Talia had been tempted to tell her the truth. 'Not in my family it doesn't,' she'd almost said. 'The only detail my mother ever worried about was getting married *before* her pregnancy showed. And my father's only thought was how long it would take before she wouldn't give a damn if he left and never came back.'

But she'd simply laughed and spouted some nonsense about preparing for every possible contingency. Which was what she always did, she reminded herself as she started down the stairs. It was one of the reasons why she had nothing to worry about tonight.

What could possibly go wrong?

An hour later, she breathed a sigh of relief. The cocktail party was in full swing, and it was going as smoothly as silk. Talia made a cursory appearance, just long enough to check the trays of hors-d'oeuvre and the stock at the bar. The Miller executives seemed to be having a great time. They'd been subdued at first, standing in little clusters, talking quietly. Every now and then, an anxious face would turn to the doorway. But as time passed and they sipped their drinks, their inhibitions fell away and the level of noise and laughter grew.

On her second trip through the ballroom, Talia overheard a snatch of conversation that confirmed what she had already suspected. 'Maybe we'll luck out,' one man said to another. 'Maybe the old man's been detained in New York.'

Talia breathed a sigh of relief as she pushed open the swinging door that led back to the kitchen. So, Logan Miller hadn't shown yet. Maybe that explained why things were going so well. Everything was moving along as she'd planned—even though they were one server short. Her assistant hadn't complained about it, but of course Talia knew they were.

She'd been watching for the man she'd had the run-in with earlier, and he hadn't shown up. It was just as well. If he'd been there——

'Oof! Sorry, Talia, I didn't see you there.'

The *saucier* had stepped down hard on her foot. Talia smiled determinedly. 'My fault,' she said, taking a step back. 'I'll just——' She whirled around as a pot clattered to the tile floor. 'Sorry,' she said quickly. 'I didn't mean...'

The head chef looked at her. 'Sounds like there's a pretty good party going on out there. Why don't you go have a drink or something?'

Talia laughed and shook her head. 'Not me. I'm just the hired help—they don't want me crashing their party.'

He sighed. 'Listen, boss, I'm trying to do this diplomatically but the truth is, you're in the way. We'd all be grateful if you'd skedaddle. We'll yell if we run into trouble.'

She nodded. It was a nice thing to say, but trouble was highly unlikely. The staff were efficient and well trained, and they didn't need her underfoot. Her job was planning and co-ordinating; the chef was right, she really was in the way right now.

Talia smiled, snatched a cracker from a tray as it went by, and walked to the door. 'Call if you need me,' she said, and she stepped out into the dusk.

She felt as if she'd walked into another world. The noise of the kitchen vanished, replaced instantly by the silence of the soft September evening. A breeze carried up from the sand, fragrant with the rich scents of the Pacific, mingling with the clean tang of pine drifting down from the rounded hills that rose behind the inn. Talia stood still for a moment, face lifted to the sky, and then she began walking slowly along the gravel path that wound uphill, through the pines to the grove of red-woods towering beyond them.

It was hard going, thanks to the pitch of the land and the height of her grey suede heels, but she decided to make the best of it. For starters, the air smelled too sweet and fresh to go back inside. For another—for another, she was just as glad to put off the time she'd have to check things again. For all she knew, the man she'd met this afternoon might have changed his mind and shown up to work, and she didn't really want to face him again. It was silly, but that was the way she felt.

And then there was Logan Miller. She knew what to expect there—his letters, and now the attitude of his employees, had prepared her for the worst. Still, she'd done the job he'd asked of her, and so far she seemed to have done it well. Miller would have to be satisfied, which meant that her boss would be, too. Her promotion would be rock-solid.

In a couple of years, if all went as planned, she'd have enough money saved and enough experience under her belt to start a small catering firm of her own. It was something she'd thought about and planned for a very long time. And then she'd have everything she wanted: she wouldn't need anyone or anything any more.

If she owed her mother's memory anything, she sometimes thought, it was that her very irresponsibility had been a kind of legacy.

'You are the most determined young woman, Talia,' John Diamond had once said, and he'd laughed. 'Did you learn that at Cornell?'

No, she'd thought, I learned it when Grams told me the circumstances of my birth. But she hadn't said that, of course, she'd simply smiled and said she'd learned all kinds of things at university.

The path had grown steep. Talia stopped, drew in a deep breath, and looked over her shoulder. The inn was barely visible, half-hidden by the pine trees. She should really go back, she thought. The cocktail hour would be over soon, and dinner would be starting. You could never tell what might happen then. Once, she'd seen someone take a bite of something, gasp, and fall to the floor in an allergic attack. Only quick thinking on the part of one of the servers had saved the woman's life.

She thought again of the man in the kitchen. Where was he tonight? Not that she cared, one way or the other. It was just that he'd looked as if he could have used the few dollars he'd have earned this evening. Well, that wasn't really accurate. There'd been something about him, an aura she just couldn't nail down that had seemed to overwhelm everything else. He'd looked like a beach bum, yes, but there'd been more to him than that.

She clucked her tongue in annoyance. What was the matter with her? She was tired, that was it, and why wouldn't she be? She'd flown in early this morning and she hadn't stopped since. This walk had revived her a bit, she had to admit that. All right, she'd go in a little further, just into the redwood grove ahead, although it did look awfully dark and gloomy and . . .

She heard the footfalls behind her just as she reached the first stand of giant trees. Footfalls? No, not that. Something was pounding hard along the gravel path behind her. And it was breathing hard. In the silence of the evening, the sound of air being drawn in an out of its lungs was raspingly loud.

Her heart constricted. Talia had grown up in a small city back East, and had spent the last few years in San Francisco. The closest she'd come to country living was the four years she'd spent at Cornell University in New York State, and although the campus was in a beautiful outdoors setting it hardly qualified as wilderness.

Images of bears, cougars, or something even worse jostled each other for attention in her mind. She stood rooted to the gravel path, trying to decide whether it was wiser to turn and face what was coming or to head further into the artificial night of the redwood forest. Face it, she thought. But, just as she turned, the creature that was pursuing her ran her down.

It came at her quickly, a dark blur that rounded the bend and entered the trees with a speed that sent it crashing into her. Talia felt the jarring slap of muscle against flesh, caught the sharp tang of salt and something muskier, and then she went down in a tumble of limbs and grey flannel.

'For God's sake, woman, what the hell were you doing?'

The thing that had run her over had a voice. Relief flooded through her as she realised that it was a man—a very sweaty, irritable one, from the feel and sound of him—and then she felt her own anger rising.

Talia pushed at his chest as he lay above her. 'Will you get off me?' she demanded. 'Dammit, where do you think you are?'

The man caught her wrists as she flailed at him. 'That's it,' he said, 'add insult to injury. It isn't enough you were playing statues in the middle of the path——'

'This is a walking path, not a running path. Why weren't you watching where you were going?'

The torrent of words halted as she stared into the face poised above hers. It was dark in the redwood grove; the man's face was striped with shadow. But there was no mistaking the thatch of sun-streaked hair that fell across his forehead or the darkly blazing eyes set above those high cheekbones.

Talia's heartbeat stumbled. The man straddling her was the surfer-cum-waiter she'd met in the kitchen earlier.

He seemed to recognise her at the same moment. A smile curved across his mouth, then vanished. He sat back a little so that she felt the weight of him against her thighs. 'We meet again,' he said, and she flushed.

'Let me up.'

The smile came again. 'Ask nicely.'

Talia gritted her teeth. 'I said——'

'Perhaps you didn't hear me. I told you to ask nicely.'

'Dammit! Get up. Are you deaf?'

He laughed coolly. 'I'm just not good at taking orders. I've been told it's my major failing.' The grasp on her wrists tightened. 'Now ask politely if you want me to get off you.'

'Damn you...'

He smiled. 'Actually,' he said softly, shifting his body against hers, 'I'm rather comfortable where I am.'

Talia closed her eyes, then opened them again. He was watching her narrowly, the smile twisted across his mouth. She was a long way from the inn, she thought suddenly, and a chill raced along her spine.

She swallowed. 'All right.' Her voice was wooden. 'Get up. Please.'

He hesitated. Then, in one fluid motion, he let go her wrists, rose to his feet, and held out his hand. Talia looked at it, then at him, and turned her face away. She got to her feet stiffly, wincing as she did.

The man moved quickly. His arm slid around her waist. 'Are you hurt?'

'No. I'm fine, no thanks to you.'

She tried stepping away from him, but his arm tightened around her. The smell of salt and musk came again, and she realised suddenly that it was him she was smelling, a sensual combination of sweat and some male essence that emanated from him.

'Don't be so bloody stubborn,' he said. 'Tell me what's wrong. Is it your ankle?'

She shook her head. 'I—I don't think so, no. I just broke my heel, that's all.' Her eyes met his and she saw once again that dark intensity that she'd seen that afternoon. Her breath caught. 'Let go of me.' She waited a moment, then swallowed. 'Please.'

'I'll help you back to the inn,' he said. 'Lean on me.'

His arm curved around her, moulding her to the muscular strength of his body. He was wearing the same T-shirt and shorts she'd seen him in earlier; both were soaked and clung to him like a second skin. She stumbled as he drew her to him; when she reached out to steady herself, her hand fell on his arm. His skin was warm and damp, taut under her fingers, the muscles beneath hard and powerful. Talia's pulse leaped crazily, and she pulled back as if she'd touched her hand to a hot stove.

'No.' Her voice sounded ragged, and she swallowed. 'No,' she repeated, more evenly this time. 'I'm fine. If you'd just——'

'What are you going to do, walk back barefoot? Dammit, let me help you.'

Suddenly, his very nearness seemed to overwhelm her. There was a strange constriction in her chest; her head was reeling. In all her carefully ordered life, she had never felt the confusion this man seemed to inspire. 'Just get your hands off me,' she said. 'Do you hear me? I swear, if you don't ...'

He grew very still. 'If I don't?'

Talia swallowed. 'I'll—I'll report you. I'll—I'll...'

The man clasped her by the shoulders and forced her to face him. 'I saw the way you looked at me today,' he said softly. 'You liked what you saw, Miss Roberts. But you were damned determined not to admit it.'

Colour flooded her cheeks. 'You flatter yourself.'

He laughed. 'Do I?'

In the second before he kissed her, Talia knew what he was going to do. But there was no time to stop him— he pulled her into his arms with a speed that took her breath away. One hand tangled in her hair, tilting her head back, while the other cupped her chin.

'No.' Panic turned her voice thready. 'Don't——'

His mouth silenced her. Talia raised her hands and slammed them against his chest, but he only shifted her more closely against him, imprisoning her with his strength. His mouth moved on hers, hard and deliberate, and gradually he forced her lips to open to the demand of his. His kiss became an invasion of her senses: she tasted his heat, felt the mockery of passion his tongue made as it sought hers.

The assault of his embrace flamed through her, scorching a path the length of her body. Talia grew still in the stranger's arms; her lashes fell to her cheeks as a strange lethargy spread through her. She swayed in his arms and he murmured something incomprehensible against her mouth, his kiss gentling, deepening.

His hand slid to her waist, and she felt the light press of his fingers just beneath her breast. For a tick of eternity, she felt abandoned by time and reality. A nameless fear welled within her, more of herself than of him.

With a sob of desperation, Talia pushed hard against his chest and twisted free of his embrace.

'Are you always this brave,' she said, after her heart had stopped racing, 'or is it because I'm a woman that you think you can take what you want?'

He laughed. 'If you mean do I always get what I want, the answer is yes.'

His voice was harsh, his tone contemptuous, and Talia thought she'd never hated anyone as she hated him. Anger fuelled her courage. 'Then this will be the first time you don't.'

'There's always a way, Talia.' His eyes were cool as they moved over her. 'Haven't I just proved that?'

Her hand was a blur as it rose between them, but he was faster. He caught her wrist before she could strike him, his fingers curving tightly around the slender bones, and she drew a sharp breath.

'Let go of me. Do you hear me? I——'

Laughter drifted towards them. There was the sound of feet scuffling on the gravel path, and suddenly a young couple stepped into the redwood grove. Talia recognised the boy—he was one of the servers she'd hired, and from the way she was dressed the girl was, too.

The couple's laughter faded and they stood staring at Talia and the man. The little tableau remained still and silent and then, suddenly, he let go of Talia's hand and stepped back.

'Until we meet again, Talia,' he said softly, and then he turned to the boy. 'Help Miss Roberts to the inn. She's had an accident.'

The couple sprang apart, the boy moving quickly to Talia's side. 'Yes, sir.'

Talia shook her head. 'I'm fine. It's only my shoe. I ...'

Her words trailed away as the man turned and began running easily down the path. 'Sir', the boy had said, the word taut with deference. A little while before, it would have seemed ludicrous that anyone would address a man wearing T-shirt, frayed shorts and scuffed running shoes with such respect. But the stranger's tone and

bearing had suddenly commanded it. 'Until we meet
again,' he'd said.

The breath caught in Talia's throat. Suddenly, she
knew beyond doubt that they would.

CHAPTER TWO

JOHN DIAMOND examined the tray before him as if the chicken pieces laid out on it might suddenly spring up and attack him. 'What did you call this stuff?' he asked, picking up the serving fork and gingerly moving aside a pineapple ring.

Talia smiled. '*I* didn't call it anything,' she said, watching as he put some chicken on his plate and cut into it. 'It's labelled batch number seven—although the kitchen staff's been calling it Chicken Hawaiian.'

John put his fork to his mouth, chewed slowly, then swallowed and made a face. 'How about calling it a mistake and letting it go at that?' he said, pushing his plate aside and taking a long sip from a glass of iced water. 'Much too sweet—nobody wants anything that sugary today.' He glanced towards the closed door that connected the executive dining-room to the kitchen. 'What's next? Or don't I want to know?'

'Something involving artichokes, fillet of sole and capers.' Her boss rolled his eyes and Talia laughed softly. 'Well, you asked Staff to come up with some exotic offerings, John.'

'Remind me to tell them exotic doesn't mean inedible, hmm?' John's mouth drew up in a good-humoured smile. 'What the hell, that's what our monthly Surprise Luncheon is for, isn't it? Better to test out new concoctions on ourselves than on our clients. And we average far more successes than failures.' He took another sip of water, then set down his glass and looked at Talia. 'Speaking of successes, I've had glowing reports about the Miller Weekend.'

Talia looked up. 'I meant to thank you for sending me a copy of the letter from the inn,' she said. 'I'm glad they thought it went well.'

Her boss shook his head. 'Not just the inn. I had a letter from Miller himself yesterday.' He paused as the connecting door swung open and a waitress appeared bearing a covered platter. John sniffed as she set it down and took off the cover, and then he sighed. 'Capers and artichokes, hmm? Do us a favour, Ann. Ask the kitchen to send out a couple of omelettes, will you? Thanks.' He waited until the girl had hurried off, and then he covered the offending dish and shoved it aside. 'You win some and lose some, I guess.'

Talia leaned forward. 'You heard from Logan Miller?'

Her boss nodded. 'Yeah. The big man himself.' He looked at her and smiled. 'He was impressed. Very impressed. Good food, good service, everything planned to the last detail...'

'As if he'd know,' she said impatiently. 'I told you, he never showed up. Well, I suppose he did, I know he was listed as speaker at their general meeting and as chairman at some workshop, but I never laid eyes on him. He wasn't at the cocktail party Friday evening or the dinner either night or——'

'No one ever introduced you, you mean.'

Talia shook her head. 'He wasn't there, John. You could tell from the way people were acting.'

'Didn't you say you only made cursory appearances each evening?'

'I followed company policy,' Talia said defensively. 'Stay in the background, be available if needed——'

John held his hands up. 'For heaven's sake, I wasn't criticising you. You did a great job—didn't I just tell you that? I'm only pointing out that just because you didn't see Miller it doesn't mean he wasn't there. Anyway, you should count yourself fortunate he stayed out of your hair. Corporate weekends are rough enough without the top brass breathing down your neck.'

Talia nodded. 'I know. And I'm glad to hear that Mr Miller was satisfied.'

'More than satisfied, according to his letter.' Her employer smiled. 'I knew you'd be pleased; I gather you worked your tail off that weekend. You looked as if you hadn't slept a wink when you showed up at the office Monday morning.'

Talia nodded as the door swung open again and the waitress brought their omelettes to the table. 'It was— it was a tough weekend, yes,' she said slowly.

John peered narrowly at his plate, then picked up his fork and stabbed at his eggs. A smile of relief eased across his face. 'Thank God,' he muttered. 'Eggs unadorned. Remind me to give the chef who cooked this a bonus.' He took a mouthful, chewed, then swallowed. 'Of course the weekend was tough. A big job, and your first solo assignment. Why, I remember right after I started Diamond's, I landed a huge account...'

It was a story Talia had heard before. Only half listening, she picked at her lunch while John rambled on. Talking about the weekend she'd spent at the Redwood Inn had brought a rush of unwelcome memories. Her thoughts drifted far from the small, handsomely appointed dining-room to a narrow trail winding through a shadowed grove of trees, to a man whose arrogant, handsome face had haunted her dreams for the past two weeks.

And that was ridiculous. What had happened on that trail had been unpleasant, even humiliating. The man had been brash and vulgar. But the only harm done had been to her ego. Talia knew that, just as she knew she should have long since put the whole incident out of her mind.

But she hadn't. She was sure she knew the reason: as soon as the man had faded from sight, she'd thought of a dozen cutting remarks she should have made to put him in his place. At the very least, she should have dismissed him on the spot. He'd caught her off guard, she knew that, and she told herself she couldn't be blamed for not reacting quickly enough to his insults.

By the time she'd hobbled back to the inn, she'd been burning with the desire to strike back at him. She'd shrugged off the concerns of the young couple who'd escorted her to the door, hurried to her room, exchanged her ruined shoes for a new pair and then rushed downstairs to begin her search for the man.

But he hadn't been there. After a while, when she'd calmed down, she'd realised that there was no way he'd have stayed around. He'd certainly have figured out that she had been going to hand him his walking papers. And he'd never have let her have that satisfaction. He might be a drifter, but he wasn't a fool.

The next day, she'd thought of asking if anyone knew his name. There was a certain camaraderie among those who drifted along the California coast, searching for the right wave or the right beach, and everyone knew someone who knew someone else. But it hadn't seemed such a wise idea. People would have wanted to know why she was enquiring about him, and what would her answer have been to that?

She couldn't have said he'd walked off the job. In this business, people did that often enough and it wasn't the practice of employers to go looking for them. Nor could she have said he'd been insolent. To do that, she'd have had to explain what he'd done, and she wasn't exactly sure what had happened to her in that redwood forest.

Besides, what would have been the point? The man had made a fool of her, but the incident was over and best forgotten. And she'd almost thought she had forgotten it, in the rush of activity that the day had brought. There had been no fresh mushrooms for the dinner salads, and one of the cooks had wrenched his back. By the time the day had ended, Talia had been exhausted and drained.

But, that night, she'd had her first dream about him. It had been filled with uncertain images. But the memory of his eyes, blazing with fire, had been as vivid as the memory of his mouth moving with fierce sweetness on hers. She'd awakened suddenly, trembling, stunned by the sharp reality of that kiss. Talia was almost thirty years old, she knew the facts of life—but she had never had that kind of dream before.

What was more upsetting was that what she'd felt in the arms of her dream lover had been more exciting than anything she'd ever felt in the arms of the flesh and blood man she'd been involved with. It had happened quite a while ago, but she still remembered how unfulfilled she'd felt after the relationship had reached that stage. She'd been lonely—that was probably what had made her seek Keith's comfort. But she'd been even lonelier when she'd found that she'd felt nothing in the intimate embrace of the man who'd said he'd loved and wanted her.

The only positive thing about the brief affair was that it had proved that she wasn't tainted by her mother's affliction. The only passion that drove Talia was the passion to succeed.

She had avoided emotional entanglements ever since. There'd been no need for them; the job with Diamond Food Services had come along, and suddenly Talia's life had been full and rich. Her career had become the passion of her life, her success the yardstick by which she could measure her rapid progress away from the poverty and desperation in which that life had begun.

Now, suddenly, shockingly, her body had betrayed her. She'd felt unclean. When her heart had stopped thudding, she'd thrown back the blankets and stalked to the shower, as angry at herself as she had been at the man who'd invaded her dreams. She'd stood beneath the streaming water for long minutes, scrubbing her skin until it glowed pink, as if the soap would cleanse not just her flesh but her mind and soul.

There'd been no more dreams—until the next night. And the next. To her despair, there seemed no way to stop them. The fantasies were never really clear, they were more like mirages shimmering distantly in a hot desert wind—but they always ended the same way, with Talia clasped in the stranger's powerful arms, her body moulded to the heat of his, her mouth blooming under the passion of his kiss.

Last night, she'd awakened remembering his words. 'Until we meet again,' he'd said. Her heart had skipped erratically. It had only been a figure of speech, she'd assured herself. There was no way their paths would ever cross, they came from worlds so far apart, there was no sense in even attempting to envisage their meeting. Talia's world was ordered and controlled; it was her safe way to face life. His—his was chaos and anarchy. It was the antithesis of everything she believed in.

Not that it mattered. She hated him. She only dreamed about him because he'd upset her—that was easy enough to understand.

Then why did she tremble in his arms every night? She wasn't even asleep when he came to her. As soon as she climbed into bed and put out the light, he was beside her in the dark, his mouth a curl of flame on hers, his hands a silken glide across her skin...

'Talia?'

She blinked and looked up from her lunch, her eyes focusing on her employer seated opposite her. John Diamond gave her a wry grin. 'I knew you'd be pleased, but I didn't think my news would bring a glow to your cheeks,' he said.

Talia blushed. 'I'm sorry, John. I must have been daydreaming. Did you say something?'

Diamond laughed. 'Did I say something, indeed!' He shoved his empty plate aside, learned forward, and put his elbows on the table. 'When did you tune out, sweet-heart? Before the request from old man Miller, or after?'

Her teeth closed lightly on her bottom lip. 'Request?' She groaned dramatically. 'Don't tell me he's planning another executive weekend. I've hardly recovered from the last.'

'Ah, ye of little faith, what do we care about executive weekends when we can establish executive dining-rooms?' John grinned. 'Your mouth's fallen open, Talia. You really didn't hear a bit of what I said a few minutes ago, did you?'

'Executive dining-room? Logan Miller wants us to set one up?'

Her boss nodded. 'That was what his letter said.'

'But I'd have thought they already had one in their Los Angeles offices. A company like that...'

John shrugged. 'I gather they're opening new offices and they want us to do the honours.' He paused, then smiled slyly. 'Actually, it's you the old boy wants, lovey. He made a special request for Miss Talia Roberts.'

Talia's pulse leaped. The weekend really had gone well. To have made such a positive impression on a new client was more than she'd hoped for. 'Really?'

Her boss laughed. 'Really.' He pushed back his sleeves, then raised his eyes to hers. 'In fact, the old man will tell you that himself in less than five hours.'

'He's coming here? To our office?'

'Now you're letting yourself get carried away, Talia. I mean, it's one thing to believe in good fortune, but miracles are another story. Logan Miller doesn't come to the world, it comes to him.'

'But you just said——'

John pursed his lips. 'I said you'd be seeing the old boy in just a few hours.' He paused, then leaned towards her. 'And you shall. In his office, in LA. His secretary called this morning. You have a dinner appointment with him.'

'What?' Talia stared at her employer in disbelief. 'I can't, John. I have a meeting scheduled in an hour. Anyway, I'd never get a flight at the last minute. And I'd have to change my clothes——'

'Changing your clothes is the only thing on your agenda.' John Diamond shoved back his chair and got to his feet. 'Someone else will take your meeting. As for flight arrangements, the old boy's sending his Learjet for you.' He grinned as he walked around the table and grasped the back of her chair. 'Pretty impressive, hmm?'

Panic fluttered its wings in Talia's breast. What kind of nonsense was this? John knew she didn't work this way—he'd teased her about it often enough, but she knew that he admired her for it, too. She was a person who believed in planning. That was the way you took control of a situation. But that took time and preparation, and her boss—and Logan Miller—were giving her neither.

'I can't do it,' she said. The expression on her boss's face made her swallow. 'I mean, I'd rather not do it this way. I—I work best when I have the chance to get myself organised, John. You know that.'

Diamond's smile faded. 'Listen, sweetheart, I'd love to play this your way. But there isn't time. Miller said he wants to see you tonight.'

John pulled back Talia's chair and she rose slowly. 'Yes, but what's the rush? The meeting can wait a day or two. I'll telephone Mr Miller and explain——'

'He's leaving for South America tomorrow. Brazil or Chile, I don't know, I'm not certain what his secretary said. Frankly, I was too busy pinching myself to make sure it was happening.' John took her hand and tucked it into his arm. 'Do you realise, Talia, that if you can pull this off, Diamond will have its first really classy account?'

'We have lots of good accounts, John. You know that.'

Her boss shrugged. 'Yeah,' he admitted, 'we've got some good stuff. But nothing as up-scale as Miller. And you know this business, sweetheart. One good client leads to another.' Diamond smiled as they walked to the door. 'Don't look so woebegone, Talia. Anybody would think I was sending you off on something terrible instead of giving you the chance to bring home a fat contract.'

Talia smiled weakly. John was right. Yes, Logan Miller had a formidable reputation and yes, she had already formed a negative impression of him—but the fact was that he'd asked for her especially because he was pleased with her work. As for preparation, the flight to Los Angeles would give her time to read up on Miller International. Maybe she could even dig up something about the new offices they were planning.

She drew in her breath. 'You're right. And I'm grateful for the vote of confidence.'

Her boss smiled. 'I knew I could count on you, sweet-heart.' He opened the door and they stepped into the corridor. 'I've arranged for a car to drive you home so that you can change and get whatever else you need. If Miller asks any questions you can't field—legal stuff, whatever—just tell him to have his lawyers call ours.' Talia's boss looked at her. 'You'll do fine, kid. You'll see. I know you don't like this last-minute kind of thing, but you've already dealt with Logan Miller and come out ahead.'

'I didn't deal with him, John. I didn't even see him.'

Her boss put his beefy arm around her shoulders and began walking her slowly towards the street door. 'Yeah, but you impressed the hell out of him. With a guy like that, that's half the battle.' He squeezed her shoulders as they reached the door. 'You'll do fine.'

Talia smiled. 'I'll do my best.'

'Break a leg, sweetheart.'

She winced as she stepped into the crisp San Francisco afternoon. Some day, she thought, she had to convince

John Diamond to find a better way to wish her good luck.

Talia sighed as she closed the copy of the *Wall Street Journal* and lay it on the seat beside her, where it joined a stack of other *Journals*, a copy of the *International Herald Tribune*, and several back issues of *Business Week* magazine. There was an ache in her temples, and she lay her head against the soft leather seat-back and closed her eyes.

She tended to get headaches when she flew—a friendly flight attendant had once told her it was from insufficient oxygen in the cabin air—but she had the feeling that the pain in her head this time had more to do with all the reading she'd done the past couple of hours than with anything so mundane.

For one thing, the cabin of Logan Miller's private jet wouldn't suffer from insufficient oxygen or anything else. Everything about the plane was plush, from the glove-leather seats to the walnut panelling. It was stocked with all the luxuries of home—not hers, Talia thought wryly, and not anybody else's she knew. Even John Diamond's handsome apartment was spartan compared to this.

'Please make yourself comfortable, Miss Roberts,' the steward had said as soon as she'd settled into her seat. 'May I bring you something? A sandwich, perhaps? Or a salad? Or——'

'Tea,' Talia had said. 'Tea would be lovely.'

Moments later, she'd been sipping a fragrant brew—'Specially blended for Mr Miller, Miss Roberts, I'm glad you like it'—from what was surely a Limoges cup. An assortment of biscuits, arranged on an antique Sheffield platter, had accompanied the tea. When she'd finished, the steward had reappeared, offering headphones, a compact-disc player and her choice of musical selections, a rolling library of books or, if she'd preferred, the latest in films.

Talia, who'd only managed to find and read one short article about Miller International before hurrying to the airport, had shaken her head. 'Thank you, no. I don't suppose you have any material about the Miller corporation, do you?'

The steward had smiled, walked to the walnut-panelled bulkhead, and had touched his hand to it. A door had slid open, revealing neatly arranged rows of materials, magazines and newspapers all chronologically organised, each marked to indicate what article contained therein dealt with Miller International.

Talia had been impressed. 'You're very efficient,' she'd said, smiling at the man.

He had grinned. 'I can't take credit, miss. This was Mr Miller's idea. He likes things well organised.'

Well, Talia had thought, settling back with the earliest of the newspapers, at least she and the head of Miller International had that in common.

Now, two hours later, her head hurt from all the facts she'd tried pounding into it. She knew a great deal about the company, but, for all her reading, she knew little more than she had about Logan Miller. He was described in one article as 'A man fiercely determined to keep his privacy', and, from what Talia could see, he'd certainly managed. The closest she'd come to any information about him was in an article that dated back four years. It had mentioned possible serious illness.

Talia sighed as she looked out of the porthole at the cloudless blue sky. Either Miller had made a rapid recovery or the writer of the article had been misinformed. A man who'd set such a gruelling schedule for his executives at the Weekend Retreat had to be in good health—unless he hadn't participated and had simply watched his people work themselves into a lather. Sighing again, Talia reached for the next magazine, one dated six months after the last.

'Changes Ahead for Miller International?' said the cover. Perhaps she could learn something here, she thought, flipping the magazine open. Headache or no headache, she had to keep reading. There had to be some thread that would explain the man before they met...

'Miss Roberts?' It was the steward, smiling apologetically. 'We'll be landing in a few minutes. I'm afraid I'll have to secure the cabinet.'

Talia nodded. 'Of course.'

'You can keep that magazine out, if you like.'

She looked at the copy of *Business Week*, then shook her head and handed it over.

'Never mind.' She shrugged her shoulders. 'It's too late for cramming now, anyway.'

The man's eyebrows rose. 'Ma'am?'

Talia smiled wearily. 'Nothing. How soon did you say we'd be landing?'

'Ten minutes, miss.'

'And then what? Will there be a car waiting, or am I to take a taxi to Mr Miller's office?'

'Mr Miller will be meeting you at the airport, Miss Roberts. The pilot's just spoken with him.' The man smiled politely. 'Will there be anything else?'

Talia shook her head. 'Thank you, no. I'm fine.'

Fine, but a little bit nervous. She sat back and looked out of the porthole again, watching as the ground rushed up to meet the plane. Who wouldn't be nervous in these circumstances? She'd only dealt with Logan Miller via the post, and both times his letters had been curt. He'd never shown his face during the weekend she'd organised; he hadn't even sought her out to introduce himself.

But he'd been pleased with her efforts. That was what he'd written to John; that was why she was in Los Angeles. The plane bumped gently against the runway. That was a positive fact, wasn't it? Talia opened her seatbelt as the plane rolled to a stop. Of course it was.

And she had some insights into the man, anyway. He liked efficiency and organisation—the steward and the periodical file had told her that. He knew how to delegate authority—look at how he'd turned the plans for the weekend over to her. Everything she'd read had said he was a tough but fair-minded businessman. A smile touched her lips as she got to her feet and walked to the door. He also had good taste in tea. A man like that couldn't be too difficult to deal with.

The door slid open and warm air swept into the plane. It was always warmer in Los Angeles. Smoggy, too, Talia thought, wrinkling her nose.

What was there to worry about? She knew more than she'd thought about Logan Miller, now that she'd tallied it up. He was probably going to turn out to be a pleasant, if somewhat intimidating old gentleman. And she, for the first time in her life, was going to learn that you didn't always have to plan ahead for things to go smoothly.

The steps locked into place as the steward stepped up beside her. 'You can exit now, Miss Roberts.'

Talia smiled at the man. 'Thank you. If you'd just point me towards where I'm to meet Mr Miller...'

'He's waiting just over there, miss.'

Talia looked across the tarmac. A dark green Cadillac Brougham stood opposite, a portly, white-haired man beside it. 'I see,' she said. 'Thank you.'

The steward laughed. 'Oh, no, miss, that's not Mr Miller.' He took her arm and turned her towards the opposite side of the tarmac. Talia had a quick glimpse of a sleek black Maserati, a car that looked more like a predator than a vehicle, and the man lounging against it, his arms crossed at his chest. 'That's Mr Miller, ma'am. Haven't you ever met?'

The air seemed to rush from Talia's lungs. No, she thought, no, it couldn't be...

'Miss Roberts? Are you all right?'

Talia nodded. 'Yes,' she said finally, in a voice unrecognisable as her own, 'we've met.'

And, of course, they had.

Despite the elegant navy pin-striped suit, despite the shockingly expensive sports car, she'd recognised Logan Miller the second she saw him. His mouth curved upward as he uncoiled his lean body and began walking slowly towards her.

Logan Miller and the California drifter who had kissed her in the redwood grove were the same person.

CHAPTER THREE

TALIA'S mind raced in circles, each tighter than the last, as she tried to make sense out of what was happening. Finally there was no choice but to face grim reality.

What was happening was obviously impossible, but it was happening none the less. The man she'd treated with such cold indifference, who'd retaliated by taking her in his arms and kissing her, was also the man who held her future in his hands.

She felt as trapped as she had on her first day at college when she'd stood alone in the hall of her dormitory building, watching as girls dressed in trendy jeans and knit tops exchanged excited talk of European travel. Talia had spent the summer at home, in Schenectady, New York; she had been decked out in a dress Grams had made for this occasion, and suddenly she'd understood just what people meant when they talked about being as out of place as a fish out of water.

Would she ever fit in here? More importantly, would she be able to hold her own in this bright assemblage? She had a trembling suspicion that the answer was 'no'.

'I want to come home, Grams,' she'd whispered into the telephone that evening. 'Please. I don't belong here.'

Her grandmother hadn't even hesitated. 'Nonsense,' she'd said briskly. 'Only cowards run away. Besides, you wouldn't be there if you didn't belong.'

The homely advice had got her through the first terrifying days. Eventually, she'd settled in happily. Grams had been right, as always. She'd belonged at Cornell; clothes and money hadn't mattered, ability and hard work had.

'Aren't you glad you didn't run?' Grams had said on the day of her graduation.

She hadn't thought about the fright of those early days in years. Now, watching Logan Miller walk slowly towards her, smiling the way a panther might smile as it stalked its prey, the memory—and her grandmother's counsel—came rushing back. Her spine stiffened. She wasn't about to run now, either. And she *did* belong here; John Diamond had sent her to conduct business.

The euphoria lasted less than a moment. This was different. She wasn't a coward, no. But she wasn't a fool, either—she knew when she'd been set up. Logan Miller had known who she was—she winced, remembering how curtly she'd told him her name, how she'd ignored his outstretched hand.

'Until we meet again,' he'd said, but there was no way she could have known what he'd really meant, that he'd planned to lead her here like a lamb to the slaughter.

The proposed contract with Diamond Food Services was a lie. She had no doubt that his company was setting up an executive dining-room, but Logan Miller would probably just as soon sign a contract with the devil as with her. She was here for one reason only, and that was so that he could bring her to her knees. The only question left was how he planned to do it.

'Miss Roberts.' Miller's voice gave nothing away. Talia thought it must be the way he sounded whenever he dealt with subordinates. He was every inch the cool executive, so secure in his power that he could afford to sound gracious. 'How kind of you to come to LA on such short notice.'

Her head rose slowly. The expression on his face made a lie of the calmness with which he'd spoken. His mouth was a grim slash above the cleft in his chin; his eyes were flat, narrowed against the setting sun. He was watching her with a kind of polite curiosity, waiting for her to respond. A cold knot formed in her breast. Did he think she was going to make a courteous little speech, thanking him for having invited her to her own execution? Or was he waiting for her to grovel for mercy and plead for forgiveness?

She was the one who was owed an apology, not he. Logan Miller had known she'd had no idea who he was. He could have cleared up her misconception any time, had he wanted. Instead, he'd let her make a fool of herself while he'd goaded her with little tortures, first kissing her as if he had the right to take anything he wanted, and now this bit of subterfuge, bringing her all this distance just to make her eat humble pie.

Talia squared her shoulders. She might have to eat humble pie, but she didn't have to pretend to like it. Go to hell, Logan Miller, she thought, and she looked straight into his eyes. 'Good evening, Mr Miller.'

She was pleased with the sound of her voice. It was calm, unhurried, as if she were seated in her office and dealing with a client. There was no way for him to know that her legs felt as if they were going to buckle any second.

A slow smile tilted the corners of his mouth. 'I take it you had a pleasant flight.'

She nodded. 'It was fine.'

'Good. I told Julio to be sure and make you comfortable.'

'He did.'

Miller held his hand out to her. 'May I help you down the steps, Miss Roberts?'

Oh, how civilised he was. Well, she could play the game as well as he—at least she could try. She shook her head. 'No, thank you. I can manage.'

His eyes darkened, and she knew that he was remembering the other time he'd offered her his hand and how she'd turned it down then, as well. She came down the steps, head held high, and paused when she reached the bottom. Logan Miller was standing so close to her that she could see a muscle move in his jaw.

'I can't tell you how pleased I am to see you, Miss Roberts.' His smile thinned. 'But then, I seem to recall telling you that we'd meet again.'

'Did you?' She smiled politely. 'I don't recollect.'

She fell back as he took a quick step towards her. 'Don't push your luck, Talia.' His voice was soft. 'Unless you'd like me to refresh your memory.'

So much for civility, she thought, while her heart knocked against her ribs. So that was the game, was it? She was the puppet, Logan Miller the puppet master. He'd pull the strings and she'd dance.

No, she thought, while her pulse steadied, she wasn't about to allow that. He was going to win—that was obvious. She wondered, fleetingly, whether John would fire her for losing the account or only demote her. But at least she'd lose with honour.

Her chin rose. 'That won't be necessary. You're quite right, I remember everything that happened.' Her mouth turned down with distaste. 'How could I ever forget?'

A cool smile moved across his lips. 'It was an interesting meeting, wasn't it? Not quite the kind I usually have with my employees, but——'

'I am not your employee.' Talia's voice sliced through his. She paused, then took a breath. 'And if you have something to say to me, I wish you'd say it.'

She hadn't spoken loudly, but the wind had picked up her voice and carried it to the pilot and steward standing on the steps behind her. She felt them stir with interest.

'Of course I have something to say to you, Miss Roberts. We have business to discuss.' Miller's eyebrows rose. 'Don't tell me that comes as a surprise.'

Talia's heart began to gallop. Her palms felt wet; she wanted to wipe them against her skirt, but she was afraid that he'd see it as a sign of weakness. 'Everything about this meeting is a surprise,' she said, looking him in the eye. 'For instance, you certainly don't look your age.'

'I'm afraid I don't——'

'I was expecting Logan Miller to be in his sixties. But you must know that.'

He stared at her, and then a slow grin spread across his face. 'Well, that explains a lot, Miss Roberts.'

'Where is the old man Miller everyone talks about, or is he just someone you invented to keep people off guard?'

'Listen, lady, don't blame me for not doing your homework.'

'I did my homework,' Talia said stiffly. 'I knew all I needed to know about your corporation and the weekend you'd planned. It was my boss who said you'd be—that Logan Miller would be...'

He sighed. 'Logan Miller—*senior*—was my father. I took over the firm four years ago, when he fell ill.'

Changes Ahead for Miller International... So that was what the headline of the unread article had meant. Talia swallowed drily. 'I had no way of knowing that,' she said. 'And I didn't know who you were. You knew that. You——'

His air of easy amusement fled, leaving his expression cold. 'Would it have made a difference?'

Crimson patches of colour appeared on her cheeks. 'Of course it would.'

'You mean you'd have been more co-operative?' His voice was silken. 'Hell, if I'd known that, I'd have handed you my business card before I kissed you.'

Talia stiffened with anger. 'You know what I mean. Not telling me you were our client was a cheap shot. It was...'

There was a stir behind her. Her mounting rage had made her forget the pilot and steward. Now, suddenly remembering their presence, she stumbled to an embarrassed silence.

Miller gave her a quick, mirthless smile. 'I'm glad to see you have some sense of decorum,' he murmured.

She felt a surge of heat rise to her cheeks. 'You're a fine one to talk about decorum, aren't you?'

'Enough!' His voice was as hard as the hand that closed around her forearm. 'I never talk business in public,' he said, and then he looked past her to the plane. 'Thank you, gentlemen. That's all for now. Miss Roberts won't need you again until midnight.'

Talia looked at him sharply. 'What do you mean?'

'What I mean,' he said calmly, 'is that there's no point in my men cooling their heels while they wait for you.' He began walking towards the Maserati, his fingers gripping her arm so tightly that she had no choice but to stumble along beside him. 'Julio has family nearby, and Bob——'

'Dammit!' Talia's breath hissed between her teeth. 'You know what I meant. Where are we going?'

They reached the car and he opened the passenger door. 'Get in, Talia.' When she made no move to obey, he moved closer to her. 'I'll load you in myself, it that's what it takes.'

He'd do it, she thought, staring at him. She tossed her head, then climbed stiffly inside the low-slung automobile. Miller slammed the door, then came around and got in beside her. The powerful engine roared to life.

Talia's mouth went dry. 'Just what do you think you're doing, Mr Miller?'

'I'm taking you to dinner.' The Maserati began moving. 'We have an appointment. Didn't your boss tell you?'

She stared at him, then let out her breath. 'Look, there's no point in stringing this out any further. I'll call my boss and tell him...'

Her voice faltered, and he looked over at her. 'Go on,' he said pleasantly. 'What will you tell him?'

They were speeding along beside the runway. Blue marker lights flashed by in the gathering dusk. It felt as if the car were gathering enough speed to hurtle into the sky. But suddenly the car veered sharply away from the runway. A fence rose ahead, and beyond that Talia could see a ribbon of road.

'I—I'll tell him the truth,' she said hurriedly. 'That you and I—that we had a misunderstanding when we met——'

His lips drew back from his teeth. 'You mean you'll tell him you cut the head of Miller International dead when he tried to introduce himself to you? That you were incredibly rude, that you tried to make a fool of me in front of others . . .?'

Talia swallowed hard. 'You're leaving things out.'

Miller laughed softly. 'I am, yes. But I didn't think you'd want to tell him that I kissed you, and that for just a minute you turned into a woman instead of a machine.'

'That's not the way it was! You're distorting what happened.'

'Am I?' He shrugged his shoulders. 'I'm only describing what happened, Talia. But we can leave it to John Diamond to decide which version he prefers—yours or mine.' His foot bore down on the accelerator. 'Buckle your seatbelt. We have about half an hour's drive ahead of us.'

Her hands trembled as she did as he'd ordered. 'Look,' she said, 'we both know the truth. There isn't any contract—you lied when you said there was. It's not fair to involve my boss in this. I mean, your quarrel's with me, not him.'

Logan Miller glanced at her, then looked back at the road. 'You're right. I have no intention of hurting John Diamond.'

'Then what . . .?' She stared at his impassive profile, and fear twisted through her gut. 'I don't know what you're up to,' she said softly. 'But no matter who you are or how important——'

He started to laugh. 'I'd never have thought you were prone to melodrama, Talia. You've even written a script, haven't you?'

'Whatever it is you've planned, you won't get away with it.'

He laughed again, the sound low and intimate in the confines of the swift-moving car. 'I know what you're thinking. And believe me, you're wrong. I've never thought of a seduction as a punishment—but if I'd wanted to take you to bed, I'd have gone to San Francisco instead of bringing you here. That way, there'd be fewer complications when I'd had enough.'

'You disgust me,' she said, her voice trembling.

'And you never want to see me again.' His voice mocked hers. 'Is that your next line.'

'Look, you've had your fun. Why don't we call it even? Take me back to the plane and tell your people to fly me back to LA. Or I can get a seat on a commercial flight——'

'Are you married, Talia?'

The question was so unexpected that it stunned her. 'What?'

'It's a simple question. Are you married?'

'No. But what does——'

'Engaged?' She shook her head as Miller glanced at her. 'Are you involved with anyone?'

'It's none of your business. You have no right to ask me things like that.'

His teeth flashed in a quick smile. 'Humour me. Pretend you're interviewing for a position at Miller International.'

'I'd sooner starve than work for you or your company,' she snapped. 'Besides, there are laws against asking personal questions of a prospective employee.'

'I make my own laws,' he said curtly. 'Now answer the question. Are you involved with anyone?'

Talia stared at him. He probably did make his own laws, she thought, and a shudder went through her. 'No.'

Miller nodded. 'I didn't think you were.' They were on a freeway now and the traffic was heavy. But the Maserati didn't slow; Talia thought that the man beside her drove as he probably lived: capably but dangerously, taking advantage of whatever openings he found. 'In fact, I'd have wagered on it.'

Talia looked at him again, then turned away and stared out through the windscreen. 'I hate to disappoint you,' she said calmly, 'but there are some women who have other interests in life.'

'On the contrary.' His tone was impersonal. 'You don't disappoint me at all. I was hoping you felt that way; it's one of the reasons I brought you here tonight.'

Had she been right about what he wanted after all? She drew in a breath. 'If you think,' she began, 'if you flatter yourself by imagining——'

'I've always been good at reading people.' He gave a self-deprecating laugh. 'At least, I'm good at it when it comes to the people I work with.' His hands flexed on the steering-wheel. 'I read you right away, Talia.'

Talia turned towards him. 'Good at reading people—and modest, too,' she said sweetly.

It was as if she'd said nothing. 'Your game is success,' he said. 'You want to get ahead, to make all the right career moves.' He glanced at her and then at the road. 'You want to make the right connections, ones that can give you a leg-up.' His eyes brushed over her again. 'Am I right?'

Logan Miller had just detailed her plans for the next several years. But, somehow, he'd made them sound sordid.

'Everyone's interested in getting ahead,' she said stiffly. 'Is there something wrong with that?'

'I was only tallying your assets,' he said with a little laugh. 'Don't get defensive.'

Talia swivelled around in the seat and stared at him. 'What, exactly, is that supposed to mean?'

He looked at her. In the darkness, the sudden glint of his teeth as he smiled was feral. 'I'll explain everything,' he promised. 'But only after we reach my beach house. I want the pleasure of seeing your face when I make my proposition.'

'No proposition of yours could possibly interest me, Mr Miller.'

He reached across the dashboard and caught hold of her hand. 'Ah, Talia, Talia, how very sure of yourself you are.'

He was laughing at her. She could hear the amusement in his voice, and it infuriated her. Whatever he was up to, she knew she was to come out on the short end of things, and she was determined not to have it happen. 'I'm sure of one thing,' she said grimly, trying without success to free her hand of his. 'You couldn't interest me in anything you said if you were the last man on earth.'

His fingers tightened on hers until she gasped. 'Don't throw down the gauntlet so easily, Talia.' His voice was soft. 'Some day, you may run into a man who'll be willing to pick it up.'

She snatched her hand away and retreated to the furthest corner of the seat. Beside her, Logan Miller laughed, then pushed the swiftly moving Maserati to its limit as they raced through the night.

His house faced the sea. She couldn't see it very clearly in the dark, but she had an impression of wood, glass, and soaring terraces. The ocean was black and mysterious under a starry sky. A shore bird called sleepily as they pulled up to the house.

'I'm not going inside,' Talia said when Miller opened her door.

He sighed wearily. 'I've had a long day, Talia. I'm tired and I'm hungry, and I want a whisky. Now, be a good girl and get out of the car.'

She shook her head. 'No.'

His voice hardened. 'Didn't you hear what I said? Don't make challenges, Talia—unless you're ready to see them through.'

Colour flared in her cheeks. Wordlessly, she stepped into the night. How far was he prepared to go? she wondered. He was angry with her, yes, and he'd obviously gone to a lot of trouble planning all this, but to what end? Surely, he wouldn't—he wouldn't . . .

A yellow rectangle of light suddenly appeared at the head of the path. Talia looked up at the smiling, round-figured woman framed in the open doorway of the beach house.

'Good evening, sir. I thought I heard your car. I've set the table in the dining-room, if that's all right with you. Unless you prefer to dine on the terrace?'

'That's fine, Mrs Hadley.' Miller took Talia's arm. 'This is Miss Roberts.' His mouth twisted with wry amusement. 'I have the feeling your appearance comes as a welcome surprise to her.'

Talia's eyes met his. No, she thought, he wouldn't force himself on a woman. He wouldn't have to. Women were probably all too eager to toss themselves at his feet. She pulled free of his hand and swept up the walk, determined not to show her trepidation. Whatever Logan Miller was planning for her was bound to be spectacular.

Hours later, staring across a candlelit table, she knew she'd been wrong. Spectacular was too puny a word to describe the proposition he'd just made.

'Let me be sure I understand you,' she said slowly, her eyes locked with his. 'You want to sign a three-year deal with Diamond Food Services, is that right?'

Miller nodded. 'Diamond will be fully responsible for our executive weekends, it will pick up the catering for my company's monthly board meetings and any additional business meals we may require. And, of course, it will become responsible for our executive and staff dining-rooms in Los Angeles and Sacramento.'

Talia swallowed. 'Of course,' she murmured, as if she understood what was happening. But she didn't. Logan Miller had brought her here as pay-back, she was sure of it. But what kind of pay-back was this?'

'There's just one stipulation.'

Well, here it was. At last they were finally getting down to reality. What would he want? A discount that would bankrupt her firm? Special treatment that would require enormous staffing additions? Or was it something far more personal, something he had already denied wanting?

He laughed softly. 'For shame, Talia. Your face is an open book—whatever can you be thinking?'

She put her hands flat on the table. 'Look, this has gone far enough. I'm sure you're enjoying all this, but——'

His smile vanished. 'My company is opening a branch in Brazil.'

'Fascinating. But it has nothing to do with me. I'm sure *Business Week* or the *Journal* would love an exclusive. Why don't you——?'

'I want an American dining-room for my top people, one that will remind them of home. I want something simple yet elegant, the kind of thing that will give our clients a glimpse of the States.'

Talia shook her head. 'I still don't see——'

Logan Miller waved his hand impatiently. 'Are you dense, woman? I want you to set it up for me.'

Talia looked at him blankly. 'Set it up?'

'And run it. You'll have *carte blanche*.'

Crazy. The man was crazy. She fought back the sudden
rise of hysterical laughter. Of all the things she'd imagined might happen to her tonight, she'd never dreamed
of a job offer. 'Me?' she repeated, watching his face.

He nodded. 'You. Well, Diamond Food Services and
you.'

'Then—the letter you sent my boss was true? You
really did want to talk about a business deal with me?'

Amusement glinted in his eyes. 'Have I disappointed
you, Talia?'

She felt her cheeks redden, but she forced her eyes to
hold his. 'What you've done is confuse me,' she said
carefully. 'But I'm sure you know that already.'

He sighed as he rose from his chair. 'I know what you
thought,' he said, walking to the sideboard. She watched
in silence as he took down a crystal decanter and filled
two balloon glasses with a dark liquid. 'You figured I
wanted to get even with you for what happened at the
Redwood Inn.'

Talia nodded as he put a glass in front of her. 'Yes,
I assumed——'

'And you were right.' His teeth glinted in a quick smile.
'At first, anyway. But then, after a couple of days, after
I'd cooled off, I began to see things differently.'

'I really don't understand, Mr Miller, I——'

'Logan.' He smiled and lifted his glass to her. 'We're
going to work together, after all. Surely we're entitled
to less formality.'

Less formality. Talia had a sudden image of him in
shorts and T-shirt, the sweat-soaked clothing clinging
tightly to his body. She looked down at the table. 'I don't
know that we'll be working together. I still don't understand why you'd want Diamond to take the job after—
after——'

'It's not very complicated, Talia. I liked your work. You made all the right menu choices, you picked the right staff, you even chose the right hotel.'

She shook her head. 'The Redwood Inn was your selection.'

'Yes, that's true, it was.' A smile curved across his mouth. 'But you didn't buckle when I tossed that hot potato at you. You stood up to me, you said you'd do what I'd requested—but you made your disapproval clear.' He lifted his glass to his lips, his eyes narrowing as he watched her above the rim. 'Some people find it hard to stand up to me. I prefer dealing with those who don't.'

'But that weekend—what happened between us...' Talia flushed and stumbled to a halt. 'That still doesn't explain...'

Logan laughed softly. 'Yes, it does. In fact, the way you dealt with me was the clincher.'

'I don't follow.'

His eyes narrowed as they focused on her. 'I'll spell it out,' he said, watching her closely. 'But you won't like it.'

A quick smile curved over her mouth. 'That hasn't stopped you yet, Mr Miller.'

'All right. Here it is, then. You responded—shall I say—ardently, when I kissed you that night.'

Talia shoved back her chair and stumbled to her feet. 'That's a lie. And if that's the reason you're offering me this job——'

'You responded,' he said, as smoothly as if she hadn't spoken, 'but you iced the fire so quickly it might never have happened.' His eyes held hers. 'I don't know what stopped you. Maybe you didn't want to let anything detract from your job. Maybe you weren't interested in tumbling into bed with a man who looked as if he spent his days counting sea shells.'

Talia's eyes flashed. 'Just who do you think you're talking to?'

'All I know is that you felt something but you turned it off before it could get in your way.' His smile was cool. 'You won't let anything get between you and your goal, Talia. You're honest about what it is you want out of life, you're not a woman who smiles and simpers and flutters her lashes when a man...' He paused and drew in his breath. 'Am I making myself clear?'

Talia stared at him. Yes, she thought, oh, yes, he was making himself very clear. He'd met her only briefly, but he knew her better than many people who'd known her for years. And he had offered her an opportunity anyone in her position would have killed for.

Then why did she feel so hollow?

'Well?' His voice was rough with impatience. 'Is it a deal?'

She opened her mouth, then closed it again. 'I don't know,' she said slowly, stalling for time. 'I'd have to figure out what you need——'

'You can decide that the day after tomorrow, when you see our offices in Sao Paulo.'

'The day after tomorrow? But I can't——'

'Don't worry about an apartment—we'll provide something for you, of course.'

'Of course,' she repeated, staring at him.

'We'll pay you a stipend over and above the salary you get from Diamond, naturally.'

'Naturally.'

Logan was still talking, droning on about the job, but Talia wasn't listening. She was watching him instead. His eyes were green—why hadn't she remembered that? Although the irises were flecked with gold, in this light. And if he'd looked handsome the weekend they'd met, then there was no word suitable for describing him tonight. He was dazzling in his dark suit and white shirt.

'Tell Diamond's attorney to contact me in the morning. We'll sign a one-year, renewable contract...'

A year. A year in Brazil, away from everything that she knew and trusted and depended on, her job and all the things that anchored her life. A year of working with Logan Miller, twelve months at his side...

'No!'

The word burst from her throat. Logan stopped talking in mid-sentence, his eyebrows rose, and he stared at her. 'No?'

Talia managed a tremulous smile. 'Thank you for the offer, but I'm afraid I'll have to turn it down. I have—I have too many other commitments at Diamond. But John—my boss—will be delighted. We have other very competent people——'

Logan shook his head. 'That's out of the question.' His voice was flat as he moved towards her. 'I want you, Talia.'

Her heart began to race. 'I told you, I can't do it. But John won't let you down. You'll be satisfied, I promise. I——'

'And I told you, there'll be no one else.' Logan's eyes were green flames. 'If you're not part of it, there is no deal.'

'But that's foolish.'

His hands clasped her shoulders. 'And when Diamond asks me why, I'll tell him that you refused to work through his company, that you demanded I sign you to a personal services contract at twice what he pays you.'

Her eyes widened. 'You're crazy! John wouldn't believe you.'

Logan smiled coldly. 'Give me five minutes on the phone with him and we'll see.'

'I tell you, he'd never listen. He knows me.'

'That's what I'm counting on. He knows you, all right, which means he knows just how determined you are to get ahead.'

Talia stared into his hard, handsome face. 'But why?' she whispered. 'Why would you do this to me?'

Something glimmered in his eyes and then vanished. 'I told you,' he said softly, 'I always get what I want— one way or another.'

Tears of frustration rose in her eyes. 'Damn you, Logan Miller!'

He laughed. 'Is that an acceptance speech?' She said nothing, and he nodded. 'That's settled, then.'

'I hate you,' she said with venom.

She cried out as his arms closed around her. He drew her to him and his mouth dropped to hers. Talia struggled wildly against him and then, with dizzying swiftness, she felt the earth tilt under her feet. She wanted to lean into him, to lift her arms and wrap them fiercely around his neck . . .

His hands slid to her arms and he stepped back. 'Hate me all you like,' he said, and a smile twisted across his mouth. 'It still won't change what happens when I touch you.'

He pushed past her out of the door and into the corridor. Talia watched his retreating figure. She put her hand to her mouth as if seeking the imprint of his kiss.

She was trembling. It seemed to take forever until she stopped. Then, slowly, she followed him.

CHAPTER FOUR

IN the real world, two days would never have been enough time to arrange for a departure to South America. But Talia wasn't living in the real world any more—she was living in a universe where Logan Miller made all the rules. At least, that was how it seemed.

The phone awoke her at six the next morning. She sprang up in bed, only half awake, knocking over a half-empty cup of tea as she struggled to silence the persistent ring.

'Talia?' John Diamond's voice rose with barely repressed glee. 'Miller just called me.'

Talia pushed a hand through her tangled hair and stared blearily at the clock. 'He didn't waste any time, did he?'

'By God, sweetheart, I've been wasting your talents! I should have been using you as a sales rep—you are one hell of a saleswoman. Congratulations.'

Talia sighed as she pushed back the covers and swung her feet to the floor. The apartment was chilly; she shuddered in her cotton nightshirt.

'I didn't do any selling,' she said, trailing the long telephone cord after her as she padded barefoot across her one-room apartment. 'This was all Miller's idea, believe me.' She tucked the phone into the crook of her shoulder as she filled the coffee-pot with water. 'Did he give you all the details? He wants our lawyers to contact his——'

'Yeah, yeah, I'll put a call through to Hurwitz and Welsch first thing so they can get the ball rolling.'

Diamond chuckled softly. 'Of course, I didn't make it easy for Mr Miller.'

Talia paused as she measured coffee into the filter. 'Meaning?'

'Well, for one thing I said I wasn't sure we could spare you.'

Clutching the phone to her ear, Talia walked slowly across the room and sank down on the edge of the bed.

'Did you?' She paused. 'It isn't a lie, John. I mean, I'm up to my neck in other things at the moment. In fact, I tried telling him that, but he wouldn't listen. But if you said the same thing——'

'I knew it was a good move. The old boy agreed to up the offer. And he came across with more bucks for your stipend. How's that for being a thoughtful employer?'

Talia expelled her breath. 'I see.'

'You see? You're going to Brazil, all expenses paid, to head up a job that lifts you—and us—into the big time, and all you can say is, "I see"?' John laughed. 'I get it. You're still too surprised to believe it's happening. Right?'

'I... Yes, that's right,' she said slowly, putting her hand to her forehead. There was a brief silence, and then Talia cleared her throat. 'John? Miller isn't—he's not an "old boy" at all.'

'Yeah, he sounded pretty well preserved. Well, why not—he's got the money for monkey shots or goat's milk baths or whatever the hell it is that——'

'You don't understand. He's a young man. We had the wrong information about him. His father used to run Miller International, but——'

'Listen, sweetheart, I know you haven't had much beauty sleep, but if you could get in early I'd appreciate it.' Diamond's voice was brusque, and Talia knew that he had stopped listening to her and begun concentrating instead on the details of the job at hand. 'You'll have to tie up some loose ends if tomorrow is your last day.'

Talia shook her head. 'I've been thinking about that, and it's absolutely impossible. I have too much work to——'

'We'll handle that this morning.'

'And there are personal things that need——'

'Look, we'll talk about all that over coffee. OK?'

Talia ran her tongue over her lips. 'I just don't see any need for this rush. If you called Mr Miller and told him I can't be in Sao Paulo until next week or the week after——'

'No, that's out of the question.' Her boss sounded impatient. 'He wants you to fly out the day after tomorrow, and that's when you'll go. Which reminds me, your passport wouldn't have a current Brazilian visa, would it?'

She closed her eyes. 'No.'

'OK. Miller said he'd take care of it. He'll have a car pick you up at nine tomorrow morning and——'

Her eyes opened. The trap was closing tightly around her, and there seemed to be nothing she could do to stop it. 'How generous of him,' she said coolly.

John laughed. 'Do I detect a growl behind that purr? Temper, temper, sweetheart. He's just being efficient.'

'He's just taking over, you mean.'

'Look, what was I supposed to tell him? "Don't provide a car, Mr Miller. Talia will manage on her own"?' He sighed deeply. 'You would, too—I know that. But this just makes things easier.'

'John.' Talia caught her bottom lip between her teeth. 'John—what if—what if I were to turn this down? What if...?'

There was a brief silence.

'Is there a problem, Talia?'

She hesitated. 'No, not really. I mean, I'm not terribly eager to go to Brazil. And I wondered—I just wondered what would happen if I said——'

'But you won't.' All the good humour had fled Diamond's voice; he sounded as cold as she had ever heard him. 'Miller was very specific. No Talia Roberts, no contract. Do you understand?'

Talia stared out of the window. Early morning light was filtering through the drawn net curtains, and she could just make out the outline of the Golden Gate Bridge in the distance. In two days' time, she'd be thousands of miles from home, in a place where she knew no one—except for a man she hated.

His mouth was like a curl of flame on hers, and his hands...

'Talia?'

She drew a breath. 'Yes. I understand.'

Diamond cleared his throat. 'OK. Miller said the car and driver are yours for the day—in case you have to clear up last-minute details. Your plane tickets will be at the airport. Oh, yeah—he said not to worry about closing down your apartment, if you don't have the time. His people will——'

Across the room, the percolator hissed and coffee spilled down the sides of the pot. Talia rose to her feet. She was becoming what she'd sworn she would not be: a puppet dancing to Logan Miller's tune. 'Three months,' she said, breaking into her employer's rambling speech.

'What?'

Why hadn't she thought of it sooner? Logan would still get what he wanted—she would go to Sao Paulo and set up the programme—but she'd at least feel she was retaining some control of her own life.

'I'll go to Brazil on a three-month trial basis. It's a reasonable caveat for both sides—Miller International and us. I mean, suppose it turns out that I'm wrong for the job?'

'You won't be. You know that, Talia. You're the best I have.'

Talia drew in her breath. 'Am I?'

'Of course you are.'

'Then do me this favour. Tell Logan Miller you'll only agree to assign me on a three-month trial basis.'

She waited for what seemed forever. Finally, John Diamond sighed. 'Is there something going on I don't know about, Talia?'

'Will you do this for me, John? Please?'

'All right,' he said reluctantly, 'I'll see what I can do.' His voice grew brusque. 'Now get yourself to the office, pronto. We have lots of work ahead.'

Twenty minutes later, just as she took a last, scalding sip of too-hot coffee before hurrying out of the door, the phone rang again.

'John?' she said, snatching up the receiver. 'Did you talk to Miller?'

'He did.' The voice at her ear was irritated, taut with barely repressed anger. 'What's this nonsense, Talia? I thought we reached an understanding.'

Don't let him intimidate you, she thought, setting her cup down carefully. 'We did,' she said, praying that he couldn't hear the sudden panic she felt. 'I was simply refining it.'

His words were softly menacing. 'Despite the possible consequences?'

'Some people find it hard to stand up to me,' he had said. 'I prefer dealing with those who don't.'

'Yes,' she said carefully, switching the receiver to her other ear and wiping her sweaty palm against her skirt, 'despite the possible consequences.'

There was a silence before Logan answered. 'Very well. A three-month trial period, renewable at its conclusion by agreement of both parties. Does that suit you?'

A feeling of sweet triumph surged through her. 'Yes,' she said, 'that's fine.'

He laughed softly, the sound as low and intimate as the early morning.

'I have the feeling,' he said, 'that it's going to be an extremely interesting three months.'

Two days later, Talia stepped off a jumbo jet at Sao Paulo's Guarulhos Airport. The flight had been long— fourteen hours from Los Angeles—but the time had passed quickly. She'd napped a little, outlined her plans for the job ahead, and immersed herself in the past history and public present of Logan Miller.

He was, she'd learned, thirty-eight years old. Until four years ago, when his father had taken ill suddenly and died and he'd taken control of Miller International, he'd been head of a major publishing firm that he'd taken from bust to boom with a daunting combination of hard work and calculated risk. Along the way, he'd taken and discarded a wife. Talia had found a photo of her in an old magazine: the former Mrs Miller, looking lovely but bereft, explaining that her husband had no room in his life for anything but his corporate interests.

There'd been no surprise in that, Talia thought as she moved slowly in the queue towards Customs Inspection. Logan was as dedicated to his career as she was to hers: it was a link between them, one he'd recognised right away. It was, in a way, the reason she was here.

Logic told her that Logan would not be waiting with the crowd beyond the barrier. This was a business day, and it would be unreasonable to expect him to take time for her. Still, once she'd passed through Customs, Talia found herself searching the people clustered ahead for a tall, fair-haired man with broad shoulders and an imposing stance. She told herself that her reasons were purely practical. If Logan didn't meet her, she'd have to find a taxi and hope she could make herself under-

stood in faulty Spanish to a Portuguese-speaking driver.
That was the only possible reason for wanting to find
him waiting.

But he wasn't there. Instead, she spotted her name
neatly printed on a small sign in the hands of a slight,
dark-haired man impeccably dressed in a chauffeur's
uniform.

'Senhorinha Roberts? Welcome to Brazil. Senhor
Miller has sent me to see you to your accommodations.
Por favor, if you would give me your luggage and follow
me...'

He led her to a black Mercedes parked at the kerb.
Moments later, her luggage was stowed in the boot and
they were merging into traffic.

Talia leaned forward and tapped on the glass. 'Are
we going to my apartment?'

The chauffeur nodded. 'Ah, to the apartment, *sim*.'

She nodded. 'Is it very far from the office? If it isn't,
I'd like to stop by there first and get an idea of——'

The man smiled into the mirror. 'To your office, *sim*.'

Talia shook her head. 'I don't understand. Are we
going to the office or to my apartment?'

'*Sim*,' he said earnestly, 'yes.'

She sighed. Clearly, they misunderstood each other.
Well, the driver's English was faulty but it was far better
than her Portuguese, which was non-existent. The only
thing to do was sit back, see what she could of Sao Paulo,
and worry about where she was going—home or office—
when she finally got there.

The streets of the city were crowded, the traffic as
heavy—maybe heavier—than back home. Concrete and
glass skyscrapers towered overhead, and the hurrying
crowds were conservatively dressed, the sort of people
who would look at home at any corporate meeting. Talia
was a little surprised: with the naïveté of most North
Americans, the name 'Brazil' conjured up for her images
of Amazon jungles and sun-drenched beaches.

'Avenida Paulista, Senhorinha Roberts.'

She met the driver's eyes in the mirror and smiled. They were near the office, then; she remembered that the new South American headquarters of Miller International were on a street off the broad boulevard along which they were riding. Good, she thought, watching the changing scene out of the window, she'd get a chance to take a look at the kitchen and dining facilities which were to be her responsibility.

She knew she ought to feel exhausted after the long flight, but she was filled with energy, without even a flight-induced headache to plague her. Flying first class had helped, but Talia sensed that it was more than that. She wanted to believe that it was the excitement of being in a strange country on a strange continent, and never mind the disquieting shadow cast by the imposing figure of Logan Miller.

She looked up as the car pulled to the kerb in front of a handsome, multi-storeyed building on a quiet, tree-shaded street. A discreet plaque identified it in English and Portuguese as belonging to Miller International.

Talia's heart turned over. She was about to enter a world he controlled, and somehow the thought terrified her. She waited until the chauffeur opened her door, even though her first instinct had been to do it herself. It was best to take all the time the fates handed her. An extra minute was better than nothing. The time was almost here. Soon, the opportunity for running away would be gone.

'This way, Senhorinha Roberts.'

Talia stepped from the dark coolness of the limousine into the bright coolness of marble floors and walls. Her heels tapped lightly as she followed the driver to a pair of lifts in the foyer. The man smiled and shook his head when she stepped into the first.

'The other, *por favor*.'

She smiled, shrugged her shoulders, and obliged. Perhaps the first was out of order. But when her escort produced a small card, pantomimed setting it into a slot marked *privado* in the control panel, then handed it to her, she understood. She was to go to Logan's private office, which apparently was located in cool isolation, accessible only via electronic key.

Talia nodded her understanding. The driver smiled and stepped back into the corridor as she inserted the card. The doors hissed shut, and the lift rose. The movement was slow, the ascent steady. But her pulse rocketed as she anticipated what—and who—awaited her. Maybe she'd be lucky—Logan would be at a meeting or away on business, and some efficient secretary would greet her, then send her off to her own office.

The door slid silently open, and she knew at once that she was in no ordinary office. A terracotta tile floor, scattered with hand-woven rugs, surrounded by pale walls hung with colourful blocks of abstract paintings, opened before her. The rich brown leather of a pair of couches blended with the warmth of rosewood tables and bookcases.

But the man standing before her dominated the room. And the glitter in his eyes when he saw her made her breath catch.

'*Bom dia*, Talia.' Logan smiled and held his hand out to her. 'How was your flight?'

The surprise of finding him waiting for her confused her. For the first time, Talia did what she'd so carefully avoided in the past. She took his outstretched hand. Their eyes met as their fingers clasped. The heat of his touch seemed to radiate through her. Logan's eyes darkened; the smile twisted on his lips. Talia's mouth went dry.

Say something, you fool. Anything.

'It was—it was a very comfortable flight. Thank you for the first-class tickets, by the way.'

Inane, she thought, inane and stupid. But Logan nodded as he drew her from the lift, and she thought crazily that he was as grateful for the banal comment as she was.

'I don't believe in saving pennies and exhausting people,' he said, letting go of her hand. 'The trip is tiring enough without being cramped. How about some coffee? Or would you prefer something cool?'

Talia shook her head. 'You don't have to bother.'

But he was already walking across the enormous room towards a wall of glass. After a second's hesitation, she followed to a table set for two.

'I hope the coffee's to your taste,' he said as he drew out her chair. 'This is my housekeeper's day off—I made it myself.'

'Yes, she thought, it all made sense. The furnishings, the private lift—these were his living quarters, not his office. Talia looked up at him as he poured their coffee. 'I didn't expect you to have an apartment here,' she said. His eyes met hers and she gave him a quick smile. 'That is where we are, isn't it? In your flat?'

He nodded. 'It seemed more practical than taking a place elsewhere. What do you think?'

'What do I . . .?'

'Do you like it?'

She looked around slowly. The room was, she thought, very much like Logan Miller himself—handsome, well to do, with a casual air that never for a moment detracted from its aura of strength.

'It's—it's . . .' She looked at him. He was watching her with an intensity that drove colour into her cheeks. 'It's very nice . . . very convenient for the office.'

His smile tilted a little. 'Yes, I thought someone like you would understand.'

'Someone like me?'

Logan shrugged his shoulders. 'A career woman, I meant. Some women wouldn't. They'd be clamouring for home and hearth. My wife...' His teeth flashed in a quick smile. 'My ex-wife, I should say, would never have been so forthright. She made a great show of not understanding the requirements of business.'

Talia sipped her coffee as she watched him from beneath her lashes. A woman who didn't understand those requirements was the last thing a man like Logan Miller would want. The photo of the teary-eyed former Mrs Miller flashed into her mind, and she felt a quick, surprising sympathy for the woman who'd been foolish enough to think that home and hearth could compete with the intensity of business.

'So.' Logan set down his cup and smiled at her. 'I take it you're all ready to get to work?'

Visions of a quick tour of Miller International, followed by a drive to her new flat, tumbled into oblivion. 'Yes, certainly,' she said, pushing back her chair. 'If you'd be good enough to tell me what floor my office is on...'

He smiled lazily. 'Sit down, Talia.'

'But you said——'

'You've just got off the plane after a long flight.' He leaned forward and refilled her cup. 'Despite the rumours, I'm not a slave-driver.'

'I've heard no rumours, Mr...' His eyebrows rose and she cleared her throat. 'I've heard no rumours, Logan.'

'Are you so eager to get to work?' His smile was cool. 'Or are you simply eager to get away from me?'

'As you just said, I had a long flight.' Her eyes met his. 'In fact, it's been a long couple of days. But you insisted that I be here today, and now——'

'If I hadn't insisted, you wouldn't be here at all. That's right, isn't it?'

Talia put down her cup. 'You know the answer to that.'

Logan looked at her while time ticked slowly away. Then he shook his head.

'You've been promoted, you've had a substantial raise in salary, and yet you make this sound like a year in purgatory.'

'Three months,' she said quickly. 'We agreed on a trial period, remember?'

His eyes locked on hers. 'Renewable by consent of both parties. Yes, I remember.' A slow smile curled across his mouth. 'We never did discuss what would constitute the conditions for renewal. Perhaps we should take care of that now.'

Was it her imagination, or was there a sudden intimacy in the way he looked at her?

'I'd—I'd rather leave that until I've been here a while,' she said. 'Then, I'll be better able to judge just how useful I can be to you.'

Logan smiled crookedly. 'We can be useful to each other, Talia. You know that.'

Silence hung between them, and then she shoved back her chair and rose quickly to her feet.

'I appreciate your taking the time to meet with me this morning. But I've a lot of work ahead of me. I'd be grateful if your driver could take me to my apartment and...'

He turned and started to walk away from her. But instead of stopping at the lift, Logan turned and climbed a free-standing spiral staircase near it, stopping on the landing above. He gestured to a closed door. 'Your rooms, Miss Roberts.'

Talia's face registered her shock. 'What?'

He smiled politely as he took a key from his pocket and unlocked the door.

'I told you we'd provide living quarters, didn't I? Well, here we are. Two rooms—bed and sitting-room, with an en-suite bath.'

She stared around her. The room they were in was smaller than the one below, but equally handsome. 'You mean—I'm to live here? And you——'

'For God's sake, don't look so stricken! My apartment is all on the lower level. You'll be alone up here.'

'Yes, but I can't——'

'Such middle-class sensibilities for a woman on her way to the top,' he said, his voice as cruelly cutting as his words. 'This level was designed to provide a flat for me and separate guest quarters for whichever of my people might need them.'

Talia stared at him. His anger, and the easy arrogance of his assumption that she'd move into these rooms, enraged her. 'Mr Miller,' she said coldly, 'I prefer——'

'I know what you'd prefer,' he snapped. 'You'd prefer to be back in San Francisco, safely planning meals for the Ladies' League.' His eyes glittered. 'But you're here, instead, and not for a moment are we to forget that you're here unwillingly.'

'If you expect me to pretend I took this assignment willingly——'

Logan's mouth turned down. 'I'm not a believer in miracles, Talia.'

Her chin rose. 'And I never signed on to be—to live in—to——'

'You signed on to work for me.' His voice was like a whip. 'Didn't Diamond show you the contract?'

'It was a standard agreement. John told me——'

Logan's eyebrows rose. 'Did you see it, Talia?'

A chill crept up her spine. 'Why should I? I know what it says. I've seen dozens of them. John said——'

'Part of your job will involve supervising the preparation of evening business dinners and acting as my hostess. Your boss assured me that would not be a problem.'

Damn you, John!

He smiled. 'Was he wrong?' he asked, his voice suddenly silken. 'Must I call and tell him he's going to be in violation of the contract before the ink has had time to dry?'

Talia swallowed. 'No. I can manage that, if you insist.'

His face grew grim. 'I do.'

'But there's no need for me to stay here. Surely there are flats elsewhere...'

Logan put his hands on his hips. 'I'm sure there are. But Sao Paulo is a huge city. And, like cities everywhere, it has its problems. I have no intention of worrying about the safety of a woman alone.'

Talia forced herself to take a deep breath. 'That's very kind of you,' she said carefully. 'But I'm used to taking care of myself. You wouldn't have to be concerned with my——'

'It's nothing to do with you,' he said coldly. 'Brazil is our host country, and it's my obligation to maintain the best relations possible. That means looking out for problems before they happen.'

'That's ridiculous. I'm perfectly capable of leading my own life. I don't need anyone to watch out for me.'

Logan's mouth twisted. 'Don't you?' He reached out and clasped her shoulders so tightly that she felt the imprint of his fingers through her suit jacket. 'You're a long way from home.' His eyes grew dark. 'And whether you choose to admit it or not, Talia, you are very much a woman.'

Suddenly it seemed difficult to breathe. He was going to kiss her, she thought, and her heart raced frantically like a wild thing in a trap. He was going to kiss her, he was going to take her in his arms and she would feel the heat of his body, taste the sweet mystery of his mouth...

Her eyelids grew heavy, her lashes began to fall as he drew her to him. Powerless to stop what would happen, she waited. But suddenly he made a strangled sound and his hands fell away from her.

'I'll have my man get your luggage,' he said in a rough voice. 'Get some rest, Talia. We start tomorrow, promptly at nine.'

He took her hand and she stared down at it as he placed the room key in her palm, then folded her fingers tightly around it. They key, still bearing the warmth of his touch, pressed into her flesh.

When she looked up again, he was gone.

CHAPTER FIVE

TALIA looked up from the papers stacked on her desk as the door to her office opened. Bianca, the young woman she'd hired to oversee the kitchen staff, stood in the doorway, a smile on her pretty face. 'Lunch has just ended,' she said in her precise, barely accented English. 'It was a great success.'

Talia sat back and smiled. 'Even the hot dogs?'

Bianca grinned. 'Especially the hot dogs. I overheard Senhor Marquez telling Senhor Miller that he was reminded of a day in his youth when he was a student in your country and he went to a baseball stadium with some friends. He also said he would be delighted to do business with Miller International because a company that could make him remember his youth was one he would be happy to deal with.'

'Terrific!' Talia sighed. 'Well, at least tomorrow's an easy day. No visitors for lunch, no dinner guests...'

'No. Just the usual morning coffee, choice of salad, hot meal or sandwiches at midday, followed by afternoon tea...'

Talia smiled. 'The programme has worked out rather well, hasn't it?'

'Well?' Bianca laughed. 'I do not think any Miller employee has chosen to miss a meal since you arrived here a month ago, Talia. And if any more of my countrymen decide to sign contracts with Miller rather than with other firms, your government may declare you its secret economic weapon.'

'You know what they say. The way to a man's heart——'

72

'Is through his stomach. So I have heard.' The young woman winked as she began to go out through the door. 'But who would have dreamed it was the way to corporate hearts as well, hmm? *Adeus*, Talia. *Até logo.*'

Talia smiled at her. 'Goodbye to you, too. See you later,' she replied in Portuguese.

Bianca's teeth flashed in a smile. 'Very good,' she said. 'Your accent improves every day. You learn quickly. Senhor Miller must be very pleased with you.'

Talia's smile wavered. 'I suppose so.'

The other woman looked at her in surprise. 'You suppose so? Does he not tell you how well you have done?'

'Not really.' The women's eyes met, and Talia flushed. 'What I mean is, I don't see him that often. I'm very busy, and he is, too.'

Bianca's brows rose again. 'But surely in the evening, after you both retire to the apartment——'

'I don't see him at nights at all,' Talia said quickly. 'My rooms are separate from his.'

'I know that. I never meant to imply——'

Talia sighed. 'You didn't. I'm simply pointing out that we never see each other after business hours. I go to my rooms and he—he goes out for the evening. I suppose he has many friends in Sao Paulo...'

Her words trailed away and the other woman laughed softly. *'Sim,'* she said teasingly, 'I should imagine he must. A man such as that would, indeed, have many "friends", do you not think?'

There was no mistaking the meaning of Bianca's words. Talia managed a smile, although it felt stiff on her lips, and she was annoyed that the implication should disturb her. 'I'm sure you're right,' she said. 'And now, if you wouldn't mind, I have a lot of work to do.'

Bianca frowned. 'Have I said something to upset you?'

'No,' Talia said quickly, and then she sighed. 'No,' she said more gently, 'of course not. I'm just busy. I'm planning next week's menus, and——'

The other woman nodded. 'I understand. *Desculpe*, Talia, excuse me. I'll let you get back to work.'

Talia smiled, but as soon as the door swung shut her smile faded. She stared at the closed door, then drew a sheaf of papers towards her and picked up her pen. She really did have a lot of work waiting; even though most of the kinks had worked out of the new dining pro-gramme, there were still some minor problems. And there were more and more meetings and client lunches to plan—Bianca helped with much of the workload, but there were always things that needed Talia's supervision.

Still, she couldn't seem to concentrate this afternoon. Words and numbers criss-crossed, grew blurred, until finally they made no sense at all. Talia sighed, tossed down the pen and swivelled her chair away from the desk and towards the window.

The street below was pleasant and tree-lined, quiet in the late hours of the afternoon. Beyond, she knew, were the hurrying crowds and jammed traffic that filled Avenida Paulista from morning to night, turning that immensely wide boulevard into the busiest street im-aginable. But here, in the handsome streets of the gar-den district, was an oasis of peace and beauty.

Talia pushed back her chair, rose to her feet, and pressed her hands flat against the glass as she looked out. Had she really been in Brazil a month? Bianca had said so, and she supposed it was true. But it seemed almost impossible to believe. The time had passed quickly, days running into days with a swiftness that blurred them past meaning. Her job kept her on her toes from morning until night; it was the most time-consuming, challenging work she'd ever tackled, and she should have loved every second of it. Why, then, did she feel so empty?

Talia sighed and turned away from the window. Everyone was pleased with her work. She'd had a call from John Diamond only a couple of days ago, telling her that all the reports he'd seen had praised her to the skies.

'What are you doing, sweetheart?' he'd said with a chuckle that had sounded obscene even over the long-distance line. 'You've got Logan Miller eating out of your hand, literally and figuratively. He loves the pro-gramme you've set up.'

Now, Bianca had told her the same thing. The only one who hadn't said anything to her was Logan himself. Well, that wasn't exactly true.

'Nice job,' he'd said after the first dinner she'd planned and hostessed in his apartment, and then he'd turned away and left. She'd watched him walk to his bedroom and close the door. Only then had she finally climbed the staircase to her own rooms. Moments later, she'd heard the all too familiar hiss of the private lift and she'd known it meant that Logan was going out, despite the late hour.

'Good work,' he'd said yesterday, when she'd seen him in the dining-room at lunch.

Talia sighed as she slipped back into her chair and drew it up to the desk. What did she want, anyway? A handwritten note saying he was pleased with her work? A medal, a certificate, a...

A smile. A moment that wasn't programmed into the work day, that wasn't part of his appointment schedule...

And that, of course, was the last thing she was going to get from him. She had seen to that, the very first week she'd been here...

It was before she'd hired an assistant. Talia spent the day interviewing applicants for the job, and she was dis-couraged. The last interview ended just as a minor crisis over the next day's menu developed. When finally she left her office, it was well past seven and she was dog-weary.

When the lift doors slid open, she was startled to find Logan waiting for her. The sight of him, in faded jeans and white cotton sweater, made her heart soar—and the realisation that it had angered her beyond all reason.

He smiled as she stepped into the living-room. 'Here,' he said, holding out a tall, frosted glass, 'you look as if you need this.'

Talia took the glass warily. 'What's this?'

'Not poison,' he said laconically. 'Take it, for God's sake. It's only a *caipirinha*.'

She hesitated. Every instinct told her to turn him down. But things had gone well between them the past few days; if he was holding out a peace offering, it would be foolish not to take it.

'Thank you,' she said finally, and she took a sip.

The aperitif, made of sugar-cane liquor, sugar and crushed lemons, was perfect: cold, dry, the taste ambrosial. Talia closed her eyes with pleasure. When she opened them again, Logan was smiling.

'Good?'

She smiled in return. 'Wonderful,' she admitted.

'Yeah,' he said, 'if I have to say so myself, I make a pretty mean *caipirinha*.' His smile broadened. 'Down here, I always unwind with one at day's end.' He stepped aside, and for the first time she saw past him to the window beyond. There was a drinks trolley drawn up beside the table, which was set, she saw, for two. 'I thought you might join me and then we could have dinner together.'

Talia ran her tongue over her lips. 'I—I don't think so,' she said. 'Thanks, but I'm really bushed, and——'

'Talia.' His voice was low. 'You know you want to. Would it be so awful to admit it?'

'That's not so,' she said quickly, turning to him. 'Why would you think...?'

The look on his face silenced her. She had expected to see that arrogant certainty she'd seen before. Instead, she saw something else, something she couldn't define.

He moved closer to her. 'Why don't you go on up and shower? My housekeeper's laid everything out; all I have to do is heat things and I can do that while you change into something more comfortable. It's supposed to turn cool later; I can build a fire and...'

So, she'd been right after all. There it was—not the arrogant look, but the arrogant confidence just the same. Logan Miller had forced her to take this job, he had forced her to live under his roof, and now he expected to force her to...to...

Even in her anger, she knew how ridiculous a thought that was. Logan had treated her with absolute decorum since her arrival in Brazil. As for the rest—he hadn't forced her to tremble in his arms, she'd done that of her own volition. He'd kissed her, yes, but it had been she who'd moaned her dark desire into his mouth as his lips had moved over hers. And it was she who still conjured him up in her dreams each night, she who lay awake listening for the sound of footsteps outside her door, footsteps that never came...

'Talia?'

His hand touched her cheek lightly as he brushed her hair away from her face. The feel of his hand was like the lick of a flame. Desire coursed through her, setting her senses ablaze. All she had to do was turn to him, lift her face for his kiss. His arms would close around her, his mouth would cover hers...

'You've been working too hard, Talia. We both have.' He smiled into her eyes. 'The world won't come to an end if you just let go for once and do what pleases you.'

Just let go for once... Desire fled, banished by a yawning darkness that terrified her. Nausea rose in her throat, and she swallowed against it. 'Thank you, but

I've already planned my evening.' Her voice was cool as she pulled free of his hand. 'I have some reading to do.'

'You have to eat, don't you? I thought——'

'Yes, I can imagine. But I'm not interested.'

Logan's eyes narrowed. 'Not interested in what, Talia? Warmth? Friendship? A little honest feeling?'

'How dare you be so presumptuous?' she said, her voice trembling.

'Or are you simply afraid to let yourself feel anything that might get in the way of the next step on that ladder you're climbing?'

'You don't know anything about me, Logan Miller. You——'

He laughed bitterly. 'You're right, I don't. You won't let anyone get close enough to learn a damned thing about you. Hell, I doubt if *you* know the first thing about yourself.'

Talia's eyes blazed with anger. 'Thanks, but when I decide I need analysis, I'll go to a professional.'

'Are you too busy to look in the mirror? Or just too frightened?'

Anger sent a wash of colour to her cheeks. 'That's absurd. Just because I prefer my work to—to...'

A terrible coldness settled across his face. 'You're right,' he said softly. 'We both have work to do. Thank you for reminding me.' Logan had turned away in dismissal. 'Goodnight, Talia...'

After that, the living-room had always been empty when she'd arrived at the apartment at the end of the day. When they saw each other at the office, Logan was polite, even pleasant. But that was the way he treated all his employees. Talia told herself he'd given up; she told herself that that was fine with her.

But, finally, something had happened last night. It wasn't anything much; she'd gone out for dinner with Bianca, to a little restaurant only a short distance away. When she'd returned, nose buried in a Portuguese-

English grammar Bianca had lent her, she'd stepped, without looking, straight from the private lift into Logan Miller's arms. The book had tumbled to the floor as he'd caught her to him.

'Careful,' he'd said with a little laugh. 'You have to watch where you're...'

His words had trailed away as his arms had tightened around her. Talia had felt the swift race of her heart, the answering gallop of his. For a few seconds, she'd let herself lean against him, trembling at the feel of his body pressed against hers. She'd heard the swift intake of his breath, and her pulse had rocketed. If he kissed her this time, if he tried to make love to her...

With a suddenness that stunned her, Logan had put her from him. 'Sorry,' he'd said, his face an indifferent mask, 'I didn't expect anyone to be in the lift.'

Talia had looked at him. He had been wearing a white dinner-jacket and dark trousers, and she'd felt as if a fist had clenched around her heart. Where was he going? And with whom?

'It—it was my fault,' she'd finally said. 'I wasn't watching where...'

He'd smiled politely, his smile the one she'd seen on his face when he walked through the sales offices: a little removed, very proper, and totally without meaning. 'Excuse me, please, Talia. I'd love to chat, but I'm running late. See you at the office tomorrow.'

He'd stepped into the lift, still wearing that impersonal smile. She'd watched as the door had closed after him and then, very slowly, she'd walked up the stairs to her rooms. Hours later, twisting sleeplessly in her bed, she'd finally heard the faint hum of the lift again. The bedside clock had read four in the morning as she'd pulled on her robe, then padded silently from her room.

Safely hidden in the shadows of the landing, Talia had watched as a light came on below and Logan had walked slowly through the living-room, his jacket draped over

one shoulder, his hair tousled. A bitter taste had flooded
her mouth as she'd caught the faint scent of some expensive perfume. Suddenly he'd paused, then turned
slowly and stared up at the darkened hall where she'd
stood. Her heart had turned over even though she'd
known that he couldn't see her. Then, decisively, he'd
turned on his heel and gone to his own bedroom.

'Talia?'

A knock on the half-opened door of her office startled
her and brought her thoughts back to the present with
a rush. Logan was standing in the doorway watching
her. His face was expressionless.

'Come in,' she said, rising quickly to her feet. 'I didn't
hear you. I was—I was busy. Please—sit down.'

'I just wanted to tell you that the luncheon went ex-
ceptionally well.'

Her face lit as she sank back into her chair. 'Did it?
Bianca said she thought it had.'

A quick smile flitted across his face. 'I'm going to
have to start giving you a commission each time a new
client signs with us,' he said. 'More and more, they com-
pliment the meal rather than our sales brochures.'

She laughed softly. 'Thanks. That's nice to hear.'

'In fact, things are going so well that we're consider-
ing opening a small office in Rio de Janeiro. Nothing
very big, mind you. Just a couple of salesmen and a few
clerical people. If we go through with it, we'll take over
a house near Copacabana Beach.'

Talia nodded. 'I've heard of it.'

Logan grinned. 'Yes, I thought you might have. The
thing is, the place is a bit antiquated—it may cost a
bundle to redo. The bathrooms have to be gutted, and
the kitchen's a disaster. Well, that's what the engineers
say.'

'You won't need a kitchen for the office, will you?'

He shrugged. 'I'm not certain. The location of the house makes it a perfect place to put up clients who are in Rio, so I'd like to have some sort of kitchen facility.'

'What you ought to do is get someone who knows kitchens to take a look. There are several efficiency galleys that might fit, and...'

Talia fell silent. The expression on his face had changed; he was watching her with an intensity she remembered from the night he'd first told her about the job in Brazil.

'Exactly. That's what I thought, too. Which is why you and I are flying to Rio tomorrow.'

She stared at him. 'Rio?' she repeated blankly.

He nodded. 'It's less than two hours away. We can be there before lunch.'

There was a sudden flutter in her breast, as if her heart were a wild dove suddenly struggling against the bars of a cage. 'What you need is a domestic engineer, not me.'

Logan waved away her objection. 'You're the nearest thing to it I have, and you're already on the payroll. I need your opinion before I go ahead with this thing.'

Talia's breath seemed to be caught in her throat. 'But your engineers already——'

'Engineers don't know a soufflé from a slide rule.'

'But Rio... How—how long would we be gone?'

His eyes moved over her slowly, coming to rest finally on her face. 'I'm not sure,' he said at last. 'It all depends on you.'

Heat suffused her skin. 'On me?'

His smile became crooked. 'If you don't think my idea will work, we'll fly back.'

Why was her heart thudding against her ribs? Why was Logan watching her through eyes suddenly gone so dark they were like the sea? Talia swallowed, then swallowed again. 'You mean the office-guest-house idea,' she said finally.

A quick, indecipherable smile curled across his mouth. 'What else could I mean?'

Before she could think of an answer, he was gone.

CHAPTER SIX

THEY left for Rio early in the morning, travelling to the airport in the same limousine that had brought Talia to Sao Paulo weeks before. Logan greeted her with a polite smile and a courteous 'Good morning' before turning his attention to the sheaf of papers he took from his attaché case. He was equally detached on board the Learjet, helping her up the steps to the plane with an impersonal hand at her elbow, suggesting she ask for coffee or something more substantial.

'I promised my secretary I'd catch up on my correspondence,' he said pleasantly. 'You don't mind, do you?'

Mind? She fought back the desire to laugh aloud. Instead, she managed a suitable smile and shook her head. 'Not at all. I brought some work along, too.'

She had done just that. But it was impossible to read the report she carried. Her thoughts kept turning to Logan, seated across the narrow aisle, his face taut with concentration as he worked his way through a stack of letters.

Anticipation of the trip to Rio had kept her awake half the night. A business trip, Logan had said, but Talia had felt as if there was some subtle purpose to it of which she was unaware. When, finally, she'd fallen asleep, she'd dreamed, inexplicably, of the mother who had deserted her when she was a child. When she had awoken, she could recall only that she had dreamed it was not she but her mother who went off to Rio with Logan while her grandmother stood by, her arms crossed, her mouth a grim line of reproach.

Now, sitting across the aisle from Logan, watching surreptitiously as he read his post and spoke softly into a miniature tape-recorder, Talia began to relax. Clearly, the trip to Rio was business, just as he'd said. The last thing she wanted was to have to try and convince him that she just wasn't interested in anything else.

Not that she didn't find him attractive. She did—what woman wouldn't? Her eyes skimmed over him. His brow was furrowed, his mouth firm. He had the same intent look he had when he examined reports or chaired weekly staff meetings.

A warmth swept through her. She had seen a different kind of intensity on his face, though, one that had softened his hard mouth and darkened his green eyes. It was a look that had spoken of desire, and she had brought it to his face. Logan had wanted her. She knew that, just as she knew she didn't want him.

It was as if a silent message had passed between them. His head rose slowly. Their eyes met and held, and Talia felt as if a jolt of electricity had crackled between them across the narrow aisle. Her cheeks grew flushed as Logan's gaze fell with slow deliberation to her mouth and lingered there.

'Talia.'

His voice turned her name into a caress. It would be so easy to reach out and touch him, so easy for him to touch her. They were alone in the cabin, high above the earth, where anything could happen. Anything...

Something rose in Talia's throat, thick as cotton wool. She tore her eyes from his and turned to the window beside her. 'We'll be in Rio soon, won't we?' she asked in an artificially bright voice.

There was a silence, and then she heard Logan let out his breath. 'Yes,' he said. She heard the shuffle of papers, the snap of a lock. 'In just a few minutes.' She turned as he rose and crossed the aisle, the same expression of polite indifference he'd worn earlier on his face. He put one hand on her seat-back and leaned towards the window. 'I've asked the pilot to swing out over the ocean and come in the long way. I thought you might like a look at the city.'

He was wearing some kind of light cologne. It smelled like fresh air and forests, and it reminded her of the night he'd kissed her in the redwood grove.

She closed her teeth lightly over her bottom lip. 'Thank you.' Her voice sounded hoarse, and she cleared her throat. 'That was thoughtful.'

'Beautiful, isn't it?' He bent over her as the plane banked; his hand brushed her hair as he pointed out of the window. 'That's Sugar Loaf Mountain—see it? And there's the Corcovado with the statue of Christ—did you know you can go to the top? The view is incredible, especially at night.'

Logan went on talking as the famous curve of Copacabana Beach swung by beneath them. But it was hard to concentrate. He was too close—she couldn't breathe without inhaling his scent, couldn't move her head for fear of touching his hand.

'Rio is a wonderful city. I spent some time in South America when I was just out of university.' He laughed softly. 'It didn't last long—I was working in the Buenos Aires office, and it only took a couple of months to convince me I could never work for my father. But I still remember the places I discovered, places the tourists haven't found yet.' He looked down at her and smiled. 'Too bad we won't have time to see any of them.'

He was waiting for her to answer, but she was tongue-tied. Say something, she told herself fiercely, don't just sit here and... She said the first thing she could think of. 'But you went to work for him four years ago. Your father, I mean.'

Logan shrugged his shoulders as he sat down beside her. 'Circumstances change,' he said. 'He was old and ill; I had no choice.' His voice flattened. 'Not that I wasn't reluctant. I was doing pretty well on my own.'

'You did it, though.'

He stretched his legs out and sighed. 'He needed me. And my wife was all for it. She said I'd been travelling too much, that this way I'd be home more.'

His words drifted to silence. 'And?' Talia said finally.

'And I was.' He laughed, the sound sharp as broken glass. 'Unfortunately, her ideas of domesticity and mine were different.'

In her mind's eye, Talia saw again the unhappy woman in the magazine photo who'd foolishly thought that she could keep Logan Miller by the home fires. No women would ever be able to do that, Talia knew, and there was a sudden wrenching pain in her heart.

The plane banked again, more sharply this time. Logan reached across her and Talia drew in her breath.

'Your seatbelt,' he said, his fingers brushing lightly against her as he closed it. 'It was unbuckled, and we're starting our descent.' Their eyes met. 'Perhaps we'll have time for a look at Rio after we've seen the house. Would you like that?'

A look at Rio—a fast sweep in a taxi, and then back to Sao Paulo and work. Nothing to have lost sleep over, you fool. Do you feel better now?

She didn't. She felt as if she'd lost something she'd never quite found. But she managed a little smile in return. 'Yes,' she said, 'that would be lovely.'

The house-cum-office was disposed of in no time at all. In fact, it amazed Talia that anyone should have been foolish enough to have recommended it to Logan in the first place.

'The building's not antiquated, it's ancient,' he snapped to the young assistant who'd met them at the airport. 'Whose idea was this?' He cut off the stammered response almost before it began. 'Never mind.

Just see to it that there's a full report on my desk Monday morning.'

Talia glanced at her watch as he handed her back into the waiting cab. They had been in Rio less than two hours. With a pang of regret, she realised that they'd be back in Sao Paulo by mid-afternoon.

But, to her surprise, the cab headed not towards the airport but into the mountains that ringed the city. Logan grinned when she turned to him with a question in her eyes. 'I thought we'd take a look at the Corcovado statue. I told you, the view's spectacular. Then we'll go to the Botanical Gardens and walk along the Avenue of Palms. And then——'

Talia stared at him. 'But what about the flight back? Don't we have to get to the airport?'

'I gave Bob the afternoon off.' Talia's eyebrows rose, and Logan shrugged. 'How was I to know we'd need him again so quickly?'

It was plausible. Still, she felt a faint unease. 'I have work waiting at the office,' she said slowly. 'Surely you must know where you can reach him?'

A mischievous grin spread over Logan's face. 'I have work waiting, too. Look, I'll make a deal with you. I won't tell we took the day off if you don't. After all, I promised you a tour of Rio.'

'A look, you said. And now——'

'And now, fate's handed us a chance to enjoy ourselves. I haven't stolen off for a day in years, Talia, and I'll bet you haven't, either.' He smiled. 'Wouldn't you like to do something for once just because it feels good?'

The unease came again, and with it a sudden quicksilver tremor of excitement. 'There's nothing wrong with planning,' she said. 'If you don't plan, you can't get anything done properly.'

Logan smiled. 'That's true enough if you're talking about a day's work. But having a good time should be spontaneous. After all, here we are in Rio, with hours ahead of us...'

She turned to him slowly. 'That building we went to see—did you know that it wouldn't be suitable?'

His face was a study in innocence. 'Are you accusing me of planning all this?'

Colour rose to her face. 'Answer me, Logan.'

'What would you do if I said I had?'

'I'd tell you to take me back to Sao Paulo,' she said without hesitation.

He smiled lazily. 'Then it's a damned good thing I didn't have a thing to do with what happened. Look, this is all much simpler than you're making it. We finished our business early and now we have a choice. We can sit at the airport, waiting for Bob to show, or we can take a look at Rio. Which shall it be?'

Talia stirred uneasily. 'That's not much of a choice.'

Logan grinned. 'My sentiments, exactly. You might as well sit back and enjoy yourself.'

The quicksilver tingle came again, bringing with it a sudden breathlessness. It was the change in altitude, she told herself, looking out at the heavy green foilage that grew alongside the mountain road—it had to be. 'I'll try,' she said. 'But I'll probably just keep thinking of all the work waiting for me in Sao Paulo.'

Logan laughed. 'Tell me that a couple of hours from now and I might believe you.'

It took less time than that for the constraints that bound her to begin to slip away. It had been silly to accuse Logan of planning this day—the more she thought about it, the more foolish she felt for even having thought such a thing. There'd been a mix-up, that was all, and they were left with time to spare. And he'd been right, it would have been foolish not to see Rio. It was, as he'd promised, a wonderful city.

The exotic Brazil she had longed for was here, in this beautiful place beside the sea. Instead of Sao Paulo's grey skyscrapers, Rio had buildings drenched in soft, sun-washed colours. Instead of crowds of faceless business-people, there were crowds of laughing Brazilians, the women lovely, the men handsome. And Logan knew all the right places to go: they saw parrots so bright in colour that they seemed artificial, and artisans working in clay and wood. The cab took them to a nearby village and they watched as fishermen worked their long woven nets. They even walked the pristine-white sands of a deserted, palm-tree-fringed beach, Logan with his grey flannel trousers rolled to mid-calf, Talia with her shoes clutched in her hand.

'Hungry?' Logan asked as she slipped her shoes on again.

'Yes,' she admitted, 'a little.'

He smiled and took her to a little restaurant just off the beach for lunch. A scarlet macaw shrieked from its perch on the veranda as they stepped inside.

The menu was long and indecipherable. Talia puzzled over it for a few minutes, then put it aside. 'I don't understand a word,' she said. 'Could you just order me a sandwich and a glass of iced tea?'

Logan laughed. 'In a *churrascaria*? That would be heresy.'

'What's a—a...?'

'A grill house. They serve *churrasco* here, Talia. Brazilian barbecue.'

'Oh, but I don't...'

But Logan was already gesturing for their waiter and ordering their meal. The only part of it that Talia understood was his request for *duas cervejas*.

'No beer for me,' she said quickly. 'I told you——'

'You wanted iced tea. I heard.' He gave her a lazy smile. 'But I decided to ignore you.'

'You can't do that, Logan.' Irritation threaded her voice. 'I know what I want.'

His eyes met hers. 'Are you certain?'

Talia drew in her breath. The simple question seemed too dangerous to answer. After a moment, Logan smiled.

'Trust me. I promise, you'll like what I have in mind.'

Moments later, Talia shook her head in disbelief as their table began filling with platters of food. There were grilled meats and poultry, fried bananas and plantains, salads and condiments, and ice-cold Cerpa beer.

She laughed. 'No,' she said, 'it's impossible. Is all that just for us? I could never...'

But, as it turned out, she not only could, she did. Some of the tastes were familiar, others were new and exotic, but all of it was wonderful. Logan had been right about the beer, too. It was the perfect accompaniment.

And, while they ate, they talked. Not about anything special—they groaned over the foreign tourists at a nearby table who thought to overcome the language barrier by talking to their baffled but smiling waiter in ever louder voices; they laughed when the shrieks of the macaw on the veranda outside joined in as counterpoint.

Talia couldn't remember the last time she'd felt so relaxed. And so happy. Her eyes swept over Logan's face. She was glad he'd insisted that she come with him to Rio, glad she'd let him talk her into this bit of sightseeing...

'What are you thinking?'

She felt herself flush. 'Me?' She shrugged her shoulders and looked down at her plate. 'Just that— that I may not eat again for the rest of the week.'

He grinned. 'Good, hmm?'

'Not good. Marvellous.' She laughed. 'Understand, I only ate all this food in the interests of scientific research. I mean, what kind of caterer would pass up the chance to investigate a new cuisine?'

He nodded solemnly. 'Of course.' Smiling, he reached across the table and touched her mouth. 'You have a spot of investigation on your chin, *Senhorinha*.'

Instantly, her easy laughter died. Once more, the air between them seemed to shimmer with energy.

'Talia.'

She looked into his eyes as his finger lightly traced the outline of her mouth. Her heart stopped beating. Desire was there, in his face, and suddenly she felt the answering beat of her own pulse. What would he say if she parted her lips and drew his questing finger into her mouth...?

The thought sent waves of heat flaming through her. Oh, God. What was happening? Talia pulled away, then fumbled for the cloth napkin in her lap. 'If we don't walk off this meal,' she said, 'I'm not going to be able to fit on the plane.'

'Talia, listen to me——'

She shook her head. 'Please,' she whispered, 'let's go.'

Logan stared at her and then he nodded and pushed back his chair. 'All right,' he said finally. 'Why not?' He tossed some bills on the table, then helped her to her feet. 'Come to think of it, we haven't seen Copacabana Beach yet.'

'Isn't it time we went back?'

He smiled. 'There's no hurry. We have all the time in the world.'

All the time in the world. She knew it was true; after all, they weren't bound by airline schedules or time-tables. Then why did it feel as if the minutes were counting down to some zero hour?

Logan took her hand as they walked. She could hardly protest—the closer they came to the black and white mosaic pavement that bordered the famous beach, the more crowded it became. Between the strollers and the street vendors, it would have been easy to have become separated.

He laced his fingers through hers and bent his head towards her. 'I still remember the first time I came to Copacabana.' His teeth glinted in a quick grin. 'I took one look at the women in their *tangas*—their bikinis— and I thought I'd died and gone to heaven.'

Talia glanced up at him, picturing him at twenty-two, and she smiled. 'Yes, I can imagine.'

And she could. The young Logan Miller must have had a wonderful time in Rio. Not that he was being neglected now. The women strolling by were beautiful, their skin tanned, their bodies lush, and many of them looked at the man beside her with frank admiration. But he wasn't paying them any attention. Talia's blood leaped with the realisation. He was too busy talking to her, watching her, saying things that made her smile.

Logan's fingers tightened on hers. 'Are you glad we stayed?'

There was no point in denying it. 'Yes. You were right about Rio—it's wonderful.'

'Then I'm forgiven for keeping you from your work?'

She looked at him, tried for a stern expression, and failed miserably. 'Yes,' she said again, 'completely. It's so different from Sao Paulo—it's like another world.'

Logan nodded. 'Sometimes it seems as if no one works in Rio. You should see it at Carnival-time.'

'Before Easter, you mean?'

'Yeah. It's incredible. Nobody sleeps for four or five days. People dance in the streets—the sound of the *samba* is all you can hear.' A smile flitted across his face. 'The city comes to a standstill, but nobody cares. Everybody's having too much—— Hey! Look out!' Logan laughed and slipped his arm around her waist as a pack of small boys tunnelled through the crowd. 'You've got to watch your step if you don't want to get run over.'

It was true, she thought—between the tourists, the beach-goers, and the pavement vendors, the street was almost impassable. Logan kept shaking his head as trays of food and souvenirs were shoved at them.

'Não, obrigado,' he said, although after a while he simply shook his head.

He left his arm around her as they continued walking. At first, she couldn't stop thinking about it. The light pressure of his hand against the curve of her hip seemed impossible to ignore—it was as if all the nerve-endings in her body were suddenly concentrated in that one place. She couldn't seem to match her stride to his—she felt the way she always did on a dance-floor: clumsy and out of gait with the man holding her in his arms.

Keith had teased her about it at the start of their brief relationship, although in the end her inability to release herself to him had exasperated him. 'If you'd just learn to let go and relax, you'd be fine,' he'd said one night after she'd stepped on his toes half a dozen times. 'But you never do.'

She'd known he hadn't only been referring to the way she danced—he had been talking about their entire relationship. There'd always been a little part of her holding back, as if some inner Talia had had to watch the outer one to make sure she hadn't done anything she shouldn't.

But gradually, as she walked beside Logan, she felt her tension easing away. He kept talking, telling her a long, involved story about Carnival, a float, and a runaway goat, and after a while she was laughing too hard to think of the press of his hand, the length of his stride or the way he was holding her. It was only when he drew her back at a street corner that she realised she'd stopped trying to relax, that she had simply done it, and that she felt comfortable and safe in the curve of his arm.

He said something and laughed, and she glanced up at him and laughed, too, even though she'd stopped listening to what he was saying. It wasn't that she didn't want to, it was just that her thoughts kept hopscotching in other directions. She couldn't remember the last time she'd had such a good time. And with Logan Miller, of all people. He was so different today—for one thing, all that arrogant certainty was gone. He was just a man. And she—she was just a woman, and soon they'd be back in Sao Paulo, they'd take the private lift to Logan's apartment...

A slow, heavy pulse began to beat deep inside her. What if he tried to kiss her tonight? What if he took her in his arms and asked her not to go up the stairs to her own rooms but to stay with him instead? Suddenly, all the breath seemed to rush from her lungs. Oh, God, she thought, I've never felt this way before. I've never wanted...

She stumbled, and Logan's arm curved more closely around her. 'Talia? Are you all right?'

She nodded, feeling as breathless as if she'd run a mile. 'Yes. I—I'm fine.'

'Are you sure? If you're tired...' He frowned. 'You're as pale as a ghost. Here, let's turn down this street. At least we'll escape the crowds and the vendors.'

'I'm all right, Logan. Really.'

But it was useless to protest. His arm bound her to him as he led her down a shadowy alley. Music pulsed faintly somewhere ahead, and suddenly a man stepped out of a doorway, holding a tray of small wooden objects in his outstretched hands.

'Out of the frying pan, into the fire,' Talia said laughing.

But Logan drew to a halt. 'Wait,' he murmured, drawing her close to him. A smile curved across his face and he said something to the man in Portuguese.

Talia peered at the trinkets. 'What are those?' she asked softly. 'Necklaces?'

Logan nodded. 'Yes. Actually, they're *figas*—good-luck amulets.' He lifted one of the gold chains and the charm dangled against his hand. It was, Talia saw, a tiny fist carved of some dark wood, with the thumb stuck up between the first and second fingers. 'Brazilians say it's the most powerful charm in the world.'

Talia smiled. 'Better than a rabbit's foot?'

'Much better.' He smiled back at her. 'After all, the rabbit's foot isn't very lucky for the rabbit, is it? The *figa*'s power comes from the giver. You can't just go out and buy it for yourself. If you do, it won't work.' Without taking his eyes from hers, he unclasped the chain and lifted it to her throat. 'This is for you, Talia.'

She felt the brush of his hands and then the chain was around her neck, the little charm lying nestled in the deep V of her silk dress. A tremor went through her as she looked down at it. The tiny fist looked pagan against the paleness of her skin, and it felt warm, as if it still carried the heat of Logan's hand.

She swallowed. 'Thank you,' she said. 'But you shouldn't have——'

'I wanted to.' Logan smiled. 'Now you're guaranteed good luck. Evil spirits won't dare bother you.'

His smile unnerved her. Was there something hidden in it? 'That's good to know. I——'

'And lovers wear it as a symbol of their passion.'

Talia's smile faded as she looked up at him. Logan was watching her through narrowed eyes, his expression intense. She knew that look; she knew what it meant. A spiral of flame blossomed deep in her belly, licking through her blood with the beat of her pulse.

'Talia.'

The one word was a question to which only she held the answer. But what was the answer? She didn't know. She wanted to run away, she wanted to reach out to him, and her confusion only made the moment all the more frightening. Everything had turned upside-down and she wasn't ready.

In the end, the only way she could respond to the question was to pretend not to understand it. 'Logan.' Her eyes met his and she managed a careful smile. 'Thank you for today. And for this——' Her hand went to the charm at her throat. 'It will be a wonderful souven——'

'Stop it.' The roughness in his voice shocked her, but not as much as the look of anger on his face. 'I'm tired of playing games, Talia.' His eyes glittered darkly. 'I'm not going to put up with it any longer.'

What was he talking about? She stared at him blankly, then shook her head. 'I don't under——'

'And you can stop playing the innocent.' The colour fled from her cheeks. 'Even that loses its charm after a while.' He reached out and clasped her shoulders. 'I've been patient. Hell, I've been more than patient. But now it's time to stop pretending. Don't look at me as if you don't understand what I'm saying. Must I spell it out?'

Talia's throat constricted. 'Don't say any more, Logan. Please.'

His mouth twisted. 'Come to bed with me.'

The bluntness of it stunned her. Come to bed with me. Not, 'I want to make love to you,' not even, 'I want you, Talia.' Just this cold statement of sexual desire as if she were an object...

'Don't look so shocked, Talia. You know it's where we've been headed from the day we met.'

'Stop it. Just——'

'It took a while to figure out what was going on in that beautiful head of yours, but finally I did. You want me, but you don't want any kind of involvement.' His lips drew back from his teeth. 'Hell, that's fine. I don't want any, either, believe me. I've had the scene that goes with moonlight and roses—I've had enough to last a lifetime.' He moved closer to her; she felt the warmth of his breath on her face. 'I understand that you're hesitant about games at the office—you're afraid it might affect your job.'

Bile rose in her throat. The beautiful day lay shattered around her like glass from a broken mirror, leaving behind only a fragmented reflection of what had been. 'You planned all this,' she whispered. 'Bringing me to Rio——'

Logan shrugged. His face was expressionless. 'I thought you might feel more comfortable away from Sao Paulo the first time, yes.'

A terrible coldness settled around her heart. 'Then— then the kitchen, wanting my opinion—that was a lie?'

He laughed coldly. 'Come on, Talia. Surely you didn't think I'd fly you all the way here just to give me your opinion on a handful of appliances?'

The hours they'd just spent together kaleidoscoped before her: the laughter and the quiet walk on the beach, the charming café and the little anecdotes... All of it, lies. All of it dreamed up, planned by Logan Miller so that he could get what he'd wanted from her all along. And she—she'd been so stupid, so incredibly naïve.

Tears of rage and frustration rose in her eyes and she blinked them back. The last thing she'd let him do was see her cry. 'I want to go back to Sao Paulo,' she said in a carefully controlled voice.

'Talia.' His hands bit into her flesh as he moved closer to her, his voice a purr at her ear. 'I've made reservations at a little inn at Búzios. The Cristalina is very private: we'll have our own little cottage on a sandy beach——'

Her hand flashed through the air, but he caught her wrist before she could slap his face. 'I was right about you all along, you arrogant, cold-blooded son of a bitch!'

'Come on, Talia. Relax and live a little. You might like it.' A tight smile curved over his mouth. 'Look, I was just proposing something we would both enjoy. What the hell is wrong with that?'

He was looking at her as if she were unable to grasp some simple truth. But he was wrong, she thought suddenly, she *had* grasped it—it was just that, somehow, she'd almost let it slip away.

'You're right,' she said softly. 'There's nothing wrong with it from your point of view—which is why I've no one but myself to blame for what happened today.' She drew a deep breath and raised her eyes to his. 'I'm afraid you've wasted your time, Logan. I——' She cried out as his fingers bit deep into her flesh. 'You're hurting me, damn you!'

His eyes blazed like jungle fire in his dark face. 'I don't like teases, lady. You'd better understand that.'

'And I don't like bullies,' she said, wrenching free of him. 'I'll call John when we get to Sao Paulo. Bianca can take over until he sends someone to replace me.'

Logan stared at her, and then a cold smile curved across his mouth. 'We have a contract, remember? Three months, renewable by agreement of both parties.'

'You can't be serious. You expect me to——'

'I expect you to honour our contract.' His lips drew back from his teeth. 'If you don't,' he said softly, 'I'll see to it that you never work for any place that has anything to do with Miller International.'

Her breath hissed. 'God, you really are a cold-blooded——'

She cried out as he caught hold of her. 'That's the second time you've called me that,' he growled, gathering her to him. 'And I don't like it.'

'Let go of me, Logan. Let——'

His mouth dropped to hers with a savagery that made her cry out. She felt the hard thrust of his tongue, the sharp bite of his teeth, and she knew that she would carry the mark of his rage for hours to come. When he finally let her go, she was trembling. Tears glistened on her lashes. 'Just what was that supposed to prove?' she asked in a broken whisper. 'That you're bigger than I am? Stronger?'

Logan stared at her. For a second, his face softened; she saw something she had not seen in his eyes before, and then it was gone. 'Call it a warning, Talia,' he said, his voice silken. 'And remember it the next time you decide to play with fire.'

She watched in silence as he stalked to the kerb and stepped off. 'Taxi,' he called, and at the mouth of the alleyway a car squealed to a halt and he pulled open the door and stood beside it.

Suddenly, a door opened in a narrow building ahead and wild Brazilian music spilled into the street. Talia watched as a couple moved into the doorway, the woman wrapped in the man's arms. The man pulled her close and kissed her. When the kiss ended, the woman threw back her head and laughed.

Tears filled Talia's eyes as she walked towards the taxi, and she thought that surely the sound of that laughter was the saddest thing she had ever heard.

CHAPTER SEVEN

TALIA glanced at the clock as she reached for her hairbrush. It was late—Logan's dinner guests were due soon. She should have been dressed long ago. But she was running late—it was one of those evenings when nothing seemed to go right. First she'd broken a fingernail, then she'd snagged her sheerest tights, and now her hair was determined to refuse all attempts to tame it.

Grimacing, she attacked the thick auburn locks with a vengeance, brushing them back from her face, then stabbing home a pair of small combs. 'You'd better hold this time,' she murmured, staring into the mirror. The threat seemed to work: the combs stayed put.

She should have had it cut, she thought as she switched on the bathroom light. She'd missed her monthly hairdresser's appointment back home, thanks to Logan's uncompromising insistence that she leave the States on two days' notice. But she could have gone to someone in Sao Paulo. Bianca would have recommended one...

But she'd been avoiding Bianca ever since she and Logan had returned from Rio. Her assistant was all too perceptive; once she knew Talia was leaving in a week's time, she might put two and two together and come up with...

With what? Talia sighed as she dusted a pale blusher over her cheeks. As far as anyone knew, her relationship with Logan was unchanged. It was his doing—she had to give him credit for that much. Flying back from Rio, she hadn't known what to expect. Logan had been silent throughout the trip, his expression cold and brooding.

When they'd landed at Sao Paulo, a car and driver had been waiting.

'Take the *senhorinha* wherever she wishes,' Logan had ordered.

'And you, *senhor*?'

His answer had been curt. 'I'll take care of myself.' And he'd turned away without a word to her.

He'd stayed away all the rest of the weekend. Talia had told herself that she wasn't listening for the faint hum of the lift or the sound of his footsteps on the level below hers. But her ears had strained in the silence of that first night and then the next.

When he'd finally come in late Sunday evening, there had been no mistaking his presence. Talia had just showered; she'd come out of her bathroom door wrapped in an oversized towel, dampness glistening on her skin, just as the door of the lift had opened. She had paused, every nerve tense.

He had been whistling. But it hadn't been a cheerful sound—it had been the tuneless dissonance of the wind through barren trees. The sound of his footsteps, instead of fading as he went to his bedroom, had seemed to grow louder. Her heart had skipped a beat. Was he coming up the stairs? Was he...?

The whistling had stopped. Talia had felt herself begin to tremble, and she'd told herself that it was with fear.

And then, abruptly, the whistling had started again, louder and even more off-key than before. She'd heard the sound of his retreating footsteps, heard them grow faint, and then the door to his bedroom slammed shut.

She'd slept badly that night, finally giving up the effort in the early hours of the morning. The street outside had been silent as she'd dressed, slipped from her room, then tiptoed down the stairs. Logan's door had still been closed, but she hadn't breathed easily until the lift door had shut behind her.

That afternoon, he'd sent for her. She'd gone to his office with trepidation, expecting—expecting what? A continuation, perhaps, of the terrible things he'd said to her in Rio.

She needn't have worried. Denied what he wanted, Logan had been interested only in a return to business as usual. His eyes and voice had been cold. 'I wanted to remind you of your role here, Talia. You are under contract to me. Until you leave Sao Paulo, I expect no slackening of performance. Is that clear?'

Relieved, she'd nodded agreement. From then on, the day in Rio might never have happened. Logan had gone back to treating her with the same removed civility as at the beginning. The only difference—one which she was sure Bianca had sensed—was that they saw each other even less than before. During the business day, Logan sent her memos rather than requesting that she come to his office. She found reasons not to attend staff meetings, and he never questioned them.

Away from the office, they might as well have been living in separate cities instead of sharing the same quarters. Talia had fallen into the habit of going to her office before Logan awoke. He was out late every night and gone every weekend.

And she knew who he spent those nights and weekends with.

Long before she'd seen the woman, Talia had known all about her. She wore a heavy, expensive fragrance— the scent lingered on the jackets Logan sometimes left tossed over the arm of the leather couch nearest the lift. She used a crimson lipstick, red as blood—there'd been a smear of it on one of his monogrammed handkerchiefs lying crumpled in the corner of the lift one Monday. She'd even heard her laughter once, late one night when the lift doors hissed open. It had sounded false, like a note struck on an out-of-tune piano.

Not that she cared. Not that it mattered one bit...

But she had lain awake for hours, throat constricted, until finally she'd heard Logan's footsteps and the sharp tap of high heels returning to the lift as the doors had whispered shut.

The next day, the woman had appeared in the office. Talia had smelled the perfume, heard the staccato footfalls, and known at once who was behind her. She'd turned quickly, just in time to see her knock at Logan's door.

It had felt as if a giant fist had caught hold of her heart. The woman had been beautiful—dark-haired, dark-eyed, she had been as exotic as a jungle cat. Talia had watched as the door had opened. Logan had risen from behind his desk and come towards his visitor.

'Darling.' Her voice had matched the sultry perfume. 'Have I surprised you?'

Logan had hesitated; then his eyes had met Talia's and a tight smile had curved across his mouth. 'Delightfully,' he'd answered. And then his head had dipped towards the woman in his arms and the door had swung shut.

Later that day, for the first time in weeks, he'd sent for Talia and had told her to plan the dinner that was to take place tonight.

'We'll be five at the table. Senhor Branco, Senhor Santos. Myself.' His smile had been perfunctory. 'And you, of course.'

'But you said five...?'

'Yes. I've asked Senhor Branco to bring his daughter, Vitoria.' Logan had looked like a cat contemplating a canary. 'Perhaps you saw her earlier, Talia. She stopped by my office at lunchtime.'

The room had suddenly seemed to fill with the woman's cloying scent.

'I don't recall,' Talia had said coolly. 'Did you have any special menu in mind?'

Logan had shrugged dismissively. 'I'll leave the specifics to you. Just be sure you plan something rather special. You know the kind of thing I mean. Cocktails first. Several courses for dinner, a different wine with each. And arrange for extra staff.' His teeth glinted. 'It's going to be a rather important evening.'

A rather important evening. Perfume had seemed to fill her nostrils again; it had been difficult to answer, but she'd managed. 'Will there be anything else?'

'Yes.' Logan's gaze had moved over her with cool disinterest, as if she were a piece of office furniture that needed refurbishing. 'Be sure you dress accordingly.'

'I had no intention of wearing jeans and a sweatshirt,' she'd said stiffly.

Logan had laughed. 'I wasn't trying to insult you, Talia. It's just that I've told my guests this is to be black tie. I simply want you properly gowned.'

Her chin had lifted. 'I'm afraid I'll have to disappoint you, Logan. I have no long dress with me.'

Logan's mouth had twitched. 'Then buy something.'

'I beg your pardon?'

'I said, buy what you need. Charge it to me.' The look on her face had made him laugh. 'To the company, then. It's a business expense.'

Finding something appropriate had been difficult. Bianca had taken her to one of Sao Paulo's finest shops, gushing over everything the proprietor had brought out, but Talia had vetoed them all. Did 'long' also have to mean backless and frontless? Finally, in desperation, she'd settled on a black silk gown with a jewel neckline and batwing sleeves that went to the wrist.

'It seems—I don't know, a little revealing, don't you think?' she'd asked Bianca.

Her assistant had clucked her tongue. '*Não*, Talia. It is most proper.'

Talia had hesitated, then given in. She had been weary of trying on dresses for a dinner party she'd dreaded attending. 'All right. But this slit has to be closed,' she'd said, indicating the open slash that went from thigh to hem.

'No problem, *Senhorinha*,' the sales assistant had said after consultation with Bianca, and she'd smiled and made quick motions with her hands as if she were sewing with needle and thread.

Now, staring into her bedroom mirror, Talia frowned. The alteration hadn't been done—how had she missed seeing that? She took a tentative step, watching herself in the mirror as she did, and she moaned softly.

Every movement was accompanied by a flash of long, nylon-clad leg. And she'd been right, the damned gown *did* cling to the curves of her body. As for her hair— one comb had already slipped free. With an oath, Talia pulled out the other and tossed it aside. Her hair tumbled to her shoulders in a dark auburn cloud. What to do? Her hair, her gown...

The ring of the phone pierced the silence. Talia glanced at the clock, then paled. There was no need to take the call. She knew it would be Logan, angrily demanding her presence. Well, she thought, so much for the way she looked. It would just have to do.

Butterflies were playing loop-the-loop in her stomach. She took a final breath, then let it out. 'Break a leg, kid,' she whispered aloud, and then she opened the door and stepped into the hall.

The start of the evening bore all the markings of disaster. Talia was even later than she'd thought: as she stepped out on the landing, she heard the murmur of voices and she knew Logan's guests had arrived. There'd be no time now to check the thousand and one last-minute details of the dinner she'd planned. If he was angry, how could she blame him?

Her high heels clicked loudly on the stairs. Silence settled on the little assemblage below, and faces turned to watch as she descended. It took all Talia's concentration to keep from touching her unruly curls or clasping the slit in her dress. Her glance met Logan's.

Something flamed suddenly within the green depths of his eyes. For an instant, it was as if they were alone. Her step faltered and she bowed her head. When she lifted it and looked at him again, she could see how mistaken she was. What she saw in his eyes was anger. But he was more than angry, he was furious—she could see it in the set of his mouth, the tautness of the skin over his cheekbones.

The woman standing beside him cleared her throat. 'Logan,' she said in softly accented English, and she put her hand on his arm.

'How nice of you to join us,' he said.

'I'm sorry. I was delayed. I——'

He gave her a look of dismissal so cool it made her flush. 'I believe you know these gentlemen—Senhor Santos and Senhor Branco.'

'Yes. We've met. I——'

'How lovely you look, *senhorinha*,' Branco said, raising her hand to his lips.

Santos smiled. 'You were worth waiting for, *senhorinha*.'

'And this is Senhorinha Branco.' Logan put his arm lightly around the shoulders of the woman beside him and drew her forward. 'Vitoria, this is Talia Roberts.'

Vitoria Branco was dressed in a flaming-red velvet gown cut almost to her navel, half exposing an upthrust, creamy white bosom. 'Of course,' she purred, ignoring the hand Talia held out to her, 'your cook. How charming.'

Logan laughed. 'Not quite, darling. Talia's in charge of our catering programme.' He looked at Talia. 'That's why she's here tonight. Isn't that right, Talia?'

He was right. But why did his explanation seem like an insult? 'Yes,' she said, smiling politely.

Vitoria's delicate brows arched. '*Sim?* Would you, then, be kind enough to refill my glass? I am drinking white wine.'

Talia's smile did not falter. 'Of course. May I offer you something, Senhor Branco? Senhor Santos?'

Frederico Branco stepped forward and took her elbow. 'Indeed you may. I should like the pleasure of your company, *senhorinha*.' He cast a cool eye at his daughter. 'Toria, surely you can find the wine yourself?'

Vitoria Branco ignored the gentle admonishment. 'It's all right,' she said, linking her arm through Logan's, 'Logan will take care of me.' She smiled up at him. 'You will, won't you, darling?'

There was a brief pause, and then Logan laughed softly. 'Of course.'

Talia watched as he drew Vitoria closer to him as they walked across the living-room. The woman's dark head was tilted up to his, she was smiling at him with easy intimacy...

'*Senhorinha?*'

She started. Roberto Santos was standing beside her, a pleasant smile on his tanned face.

'Forgive me, *senhor*, I'm afraid I was wool-gathering. Were you talking to me?'

Santos nodded. 'I was saying how delighted I was when I learned you would be joining us this evening. It is always a pleasure to dine with executives from Miller International.'

His words were gracious and, she suspected, meant to take the sting out of what had just happened. She smiled gratefully. 'Thank you, *senhor*. The pleasure is mine, as well.' She looked from Santos to Branco. 'Would either of you like an aperitif?'

Santos grinned. 'Ah, how wonderful. The lady is bright, beautiful, and a mind-reader, as well.' He took her hand and folded it into the curve of his arm. 'Tell

me, my dear, what would it take to convince you to leave
Miller and come to work for my firm instead?'

Frederico Branco clucked his tongue. 'For shame,
Roberto.' He grinned as he took Talia's free hand and
tucked it into his arm. 'Santos is as impolite as my
daughter,' he said with mock severity. 'One should never
talk business on an empty stomach—especially when such
a lovely woman is at hand. Now behave yourself,
Roberto, or the *senhorinha* will think us all barbarians.'

Santos and Branco never left her side after that. They
watched her with frank admiration, hung on every word
she spoke. They seated themselves on either side of her
at dinner, regaling her with stories about Brazil's jungle
interior. Logan interrupted once or twice and the men
responded politely, but they always found a way to turn
the conversation back to Talia. She knew she should feel
flattered by their attention. Both were handsome—'Good
catches, these two,' Bianca had gushed. Santos, a
bachelor, was about Logan's age, darker and shorter,
but very good-looking. Branco, a widower in his late
forties, was vigorous and attractive.

She told herself that only a fool wouldn't have been
pleased to be the centre of their interest. But, as the
evening progressed, she found herself glancing at Logan
more and more. She flushed the first time he looked up
and his eyes met hers. Quickly, she turned away and
smiled at Frederico Branco. 'Tell me about yourself,
senhor,' she said.

The next time her eyes met Logan's, she was even more
flustered. His expression was grim, and she knew he must
still be angry at her for having been late. And now, here
she was, paying scant attention to his guests which was,
as he'd so coldly reminded her, the job she was here to
do.

She swung her attention to Roberto Santos and gave
him a dazzling smile. 'Would you care for more wine,
senhor?'

But no matter how she tried, she couldn't keep from looking at Logan. She told herself it was Vitoria Branco she was watching. Who wouldn't be fascinated to see a spider spin its web?

But if that were true, why did her throat close at the sight of those long crimson fingernails raking lightly along the back of Logan's hand? Why did her heart ache each time Vitoria threw back her head and laughed?

Logan was strangely silent. At first, Talia thought it was because Vitoria's behaviour had him entranced. But, as the hours wore on, she grew puzzled. He kept looking at her, throwing her taut glances that were unreadable. Finally, as the little group sat in the living-room, chatting and sipping brandy, the glances became more strained until he looked like a man ready to explode.

Talia's heart tripped crazily. He was furious, and all his rage was directed at her. But why? What had she done? He couldn't still be angry because she'd been late. And the meal had gone well—everyone had said so.

A lump rose in her throat. Maybe—maybe he regretted having asked her to be his hostess. Vitoria could have handled the role; it would have befitted her new part in Logan's life. Talia was, after all, only his employee, just as the Branco woman had implied.

'...Absolutely the most—how do you say?—the most delicious meal I have ever had, Talia. How can I thank you?' Frederico Branco's words drew her back. He had risen to his feet, and now he was smiling down at her.

'Are you leaving, Senhor Branco?'

Logan rose, too. 'Yes.' His voice was curt. 'Didn't you hear me, Talia? I suggested we cut things short.'

She looked at him in surprise. 'No, I didn't. I——'

'Have I your permission to call you, Talia?'

She started at Roberto Santos's murmured question. 'I—I...' Her eyes met Logan's fierce stare, and she blanched. 'I'm afraid I'm leaving Brazil,' she said finally. 'But thank you for——'

'Leaving?' Branco's brows rose. 'But I want to show you Brasilia. Logan, surely you can convince her to stay on.'

Logan's lips drew back from his teeth. 'I've tried, Frederico, but you know how it is. Sometimes, no matter what one does, an employee is just not satisfied.' His eyes glittered darkly. 'And it's too bad, isn't it? I mean, she's good at what she does. Why, she even managed to convince you that she was happy to be here tonight, when actually it's just part of her job.'

Silence fell over the room. It took all Talia's courage to hold her head high and rise to her feet. 'It's been a very long day,' she said carefully. 'If you'll excuse me...'

She heard Branco and Santos protest, but she was already moving quickly across the living-room towards the stairs. It seemed miles before she reached them and forever until she reached the landing. A voice called after her—Santos, she thought, but she didn't look back. Quickly, she opened the door to her rooms and stepped inside.

Tears slid down her cheeks as the door closed after her. Dear God, she thought, why had Logan been so cruel? Kicking off her shoes, she padded into the bedroom and switched on the light. There was no justification for the way he'd treated her. Unless—unless he'd been waiting all this time to get even with her for what had happened in Rio.

The sudden hum of the lift intruded. Talia caught her breath, listening to the silence of the empty apartment. They were gone, then. All of them. Santos and Branco, Logan and Vitoria. It would be hours before he returned, she thought, and suddenly she could see them together, the woman's midnight hair spread over Logan's chest, her crimson mouth on his.

Talia hurried to the wardrobe and flung it open. She pulled out her suitcases and tossed them on the bed. Clothing followed, flying on to the bed in a mad flurry, and then she unzipped her gown and added it to the tangle. Packing would take no time. She'd be gone before Logan returned, and to hell with the three-month contract, to hell with John if he didn't like it.

The bedroom door banged open like a gunshot. Talia cried out and spun towards the sound.

Logan smiled lazily from the open doorway. His jacket was gone, as was his tie. His shirt was unbuttoned to the waist. There was a dark and dangerous look in his eyes. 'You left rather abruptly, Talia. You never said a proper goodnight to our guests.'

Instinct told her not to let him see the depths of her fear. She made herself move slowly to the bed, made herself reach slowly for the discarded silk gown.

'Get out of my room,' she said, holding the gown to her.

He smiled. 'That's not very friendly.'

'Logan, did you hear me? I said——'

'I heard you.' His smile twisted. 'You certainly managed to be nicer than that to your pals.'

'My pals?'

'Yes. Santos and Branco. They were purring around you like tomcats.'

'I don't know what that's supposed to mean. I——'

She gasped as his hands shot out and clasped her shoulders. He smelled of anger and brandy, and her fear grew.

'Don't be modest. You had those poor bastards going crazy. If a man didn't know better, he'd almost think you had some blood in your veins.'

'You're drunk,' she said, as calmly as she could. 'And you... Dammit, Logan!' Her voice rose unsteadily. 'Let go. You're hurting me.'

'It was a waste of time, you know. Santos wouldn't hire a woman if she were St Joan herself. As for Branco— the only thing he'd offer a woman is the kind of thing you've already turned down.' His mouth twisted. 'From me.'

Be calm, she told herself. He's just trying to scare you. 'What do you want, Logan?'

His bark of laughter was quick and harsh. He reached out lazily, his hand curving over hers, grasped the gown she held clutched to her breasts, and wrenched it from her. It fluttered to the floor like petals from a black flower.

Talia shuddered as he looked at her. In her black lace teddy, she felt more exposed than if she'd been naked.

'So lovely,' Logan said softly. 'And so calculating.'

'Get out of my room, Logan. Stop this now, before——'

His arms closed around her and he drew her to him. She felt the quick stir of his body against hers.

'Is that the way you get your kicks, Talia? Turning men on and off?'

'Stop it,' she hissed. 'Damn you——'

'The trouble is, sooner or later you're going to find a man who won't play your game.' His eyes swept over her face. 'A man who gets his fun taking what he wants, whether you're willing to give it or not.'

I always get what I want, Talia, one way or another.

'No! Logan...'

She cried out, struggling desperately as he bent to her, but Logan was on fire, burning with terrifying savagery. His mouth fell on hers with ruthless intent, his lips moving on hers with a passion that made no pretence at tenderness.

When he lifted his head, his eyes were cold as emeralds. 'Make it easy on the both of us. No more games.'

Talia felt as if she could hardly breathe. 'Please,' she said, 'I beg you...'

He laughed. 'Yes,' he said. 'Beg me. I think I'd like that.'

His mouth dropped to hers again. When he raised his head, she was dizzy. 'You bastard,' she whispered. 'You...'

He forced her backwards until she felt the press of the wall against her shoulders. Logan put a hand on either side of her, his palms flat against the wall, his arms rigid, imprisoning her with his strength.

'Why don't you smile at me, Talia? Why don't you say all those sweet things you said to Frederico?'

Tears slid down her cheeks. She had known, all along, that the dark passion she'd felt in Logan's arms was wrong. Now, the proof was all too real. The next moments would forever twist her dreams into nightmares if he...if he...

His mouth was at her throat, his breath hot against her flesh.

'Logan. Don't hurt me, please.'

Her broken whisper hung between them. Logan lifted his head and stared at her. Darkness veiled his eyes. 'Talia.'

She flinched as he lifted his hand to her, but his touch was gentle as he stroked damp curls from her temples.

'Don't cry,' he whispered. 'Talia, sweet—don't.' With slow tenderness, he wiped the tears from her cheeks. 'You're so soft,' he said. 'Are you this soft all over?'

'Please. Let me go. Let——'

His head dipped to hers, his mouth following the path his hand had taken. Talia trembled as he kissed her tear-stained cheek, her jaw, the corner of her mouth.

'Stop it,' she whispered. 'Logan...'

He hushed her softly while his hand moved slowly over her, stroking her as if she were a frightened lamb lost in the wild. She felt the brush of his mouth on hers.

'No,' she said, twisting her head away. Logan caught her chin in his hand and turned her face to him, kissing her again and again, each kiss longer and hungrier than the last.

A pulse began to beat deep within her, embers glowing in primeval darkness began to glow in her loins. Her mouth felt as if it were melting under his.

'Logan...'

'Kiss me, Talia,' he whispered against her lips. 'Yes. Kiss me. Kiss me.'

His hand slid down her throat, over her shoulder, then to her breast. She moaned as he cupped the soft weight. Beneath its silken covering, she felt her flesh swell, felt her nipple engorge as it sought his palm.

'Don't,' she said. 'Don't...'

But her body, beginning to move slowly beneath his heated caresses, her lips, parting to taste the sweetness of his mouth, turned her softly whispered protest into a lie. Logan groaned and gathered her into the curve of his arm while his hand skimmed over her, following the curves of her body through the delicate silk, then slipping inside the teddy to splay possessively across her naked buttock.

Talia whimpered as his kisses trailed across her swollen mouth, along her throat, to her breast. His lips closed over her silk-covered nipple and drew it into the warm heat of his mouth. A rainbow of a thousand dazzling colours exploded inside her closed eyelids. She swayed dizzily in his embrace.

'Put your arms around me, beautiful,' Logan whispered.

How could she deny him what she herself wanted? Slowly, Talia raised her arms and twined them around his neck.

Logan laughed softly, the sound so triumphant and primitive that it sent a racing wave of heat through her blood.

'Tell me you want me, Talia.'

Her body arched like a bow as his hand moved beneath the teddy, cupping the centre of her femininity.

'Tell me,' he said roughly.

She buried her face in his neck as he swung her into his arms, carried her to the bed, and lowered her to it. Her pulse raced as he drew back and stripped off his clothing. He was so beautiful, she thought, watching him from beneath half-lowered lashes. His body was golden, hard, aroused and eager for her.

She raised her hips as he drew off her teddy, then lifted her arms to him while she whispered his name.

He smiled. Slowly, his eyes never leaving her face, he ran his hand possessively over her, lingering on her breasts, stroking over her ribs and belly, at last finding the delicate flesh that was her core. She cried out and reached out to him again.

'Logan. Please.'

'Tell me,' he demanded. 'I want to hear you say it.'

Talia sighed, and the words she had never before uttered whispered into the silent room. 'I want you to make love to me,' she whispered.

A smile so radiant it was like the rising of the moon flashed across his face. He bent to her and kissed her deeply. 'Talia,' he said, 'Talia.'

And then there was no more time for talking. Logan knelt above her, parted her legs, and, with one deep thrust, entered her.

The world tilted, the stars hurtled across the night sky, and, for a heartbeat, the answers to the oldest riddles of the universe were all within her grasp.

But in the end, as she cried out in ecstasy, there was only one answer that mattered. She knew, finally, why she had run from Logan Miller. He was not, as she'd so carefully told herself, the man she despised. He was, instead, the man she'd fallen in love with.

CHAPTER EIGHT

TALIA awoke slowly from a deep, dreamless sleep. The bedroom was filled with sunlight, and the rich scent of fresh coffee drifted on the air.

Smiling, she closed her eyes again and snuggled into the tangled sheets. She was lying on her stomach, the blanket draped at her hips, and the sun felt wonderful on her naked back. She was sleeping nude, something she rarely did. For some foolish reason, it made her feel vulnerable. But she felt lovely now: warm, and relaxed, and...

Her eyes flew open as memories of the night came tumbling back. Logan, she thought, and she reached for the blanket, pulling it to her chin as she turned over. But she was alone in the bed. Only traces of the man with whom she'd spent the night remained in the sunlit room: the depression in the pillow next to hers, the tangled bed-linen—the feeling of sweet exhaustion in every muscle.

Warmth radiated through her body. Nothing she'd known had prepared her for what had happened in this room last night. She'd turned to flame in Logan's arms; their first coming together had been almost savage, each of them seeking the other with primitive hunger.

The next time had been different. Asleep, her head cradled in the curve of Logan's shoulder, Talia had been awakened by the brush of his mouth and the gentle play of his hands. He had caressed her, stroked her, kissed her until she had been feverish with desire.

'Now,' she'd whispered shamelessly. 'Please, Logan.'

He'd laughed softly as he'd rolled on his back and taken her with him. 'We have all night,' he'd said. 'There's no reason to hurry.'

By the time he'd finally taken her, she had been wet with her own sweat and his. She remembered crying out his name at the end, she remembered the salty taste of his skin—but, most of all, she remembered the way it had felt when he'd settled her in his arms and drawn the covers over their damp bodies.

'Sleep now,' he'd murmured. Safe and secure within his embrace, she'd closed her eyes and nestled her head against his chest, listening as the quicksilver race of his heart had quieted, and then she'd fallen into a welcome oblivion where there were no dreams. Logan had been the reason for the dreams that had disturbed, and now— and now...

Talia sat up and swung her legs to the floor. And now, what? she thought, pushing her hair back from her face. Each day she'd spent with him had made it clear that Logan Miller had had his fill of commitment—he wanted nothing to do with that kind of relationship.

She drew in her breath. What was the matter with her? She didn't want that kind of thing, either. She had her career, the life she'd so diligently planned. Some time between dinner and dawn, she'd almost forgotten that.

She got to her feet and pulled on her robe. Last night had just been—it had been sex, that was all. She'd tried to stamp it with a label marked 'love'. Maybe it was easier to call it 'love' than to admit the truth, which was simply that she and Logan were both of age, they were consenting adults who'd wanted to go to bed together, and they had.

Who was she kidding? She sank to the edge of the bed and closed her eyes. Sex was what she'd had with Keith—a perfunctory joining of bodies that had been quickly over at best and, at worst, vaguely embarrassing.

What she'd felt in Logan's arms was nothing like that. Everything that had happened between them had been natural and right. She'd never felt self-conscious, no matter how intimate his caresses. And she'd wanted his lovemaking to go on forever, to last through the days and nights and years...

But it wasn't what Logan wanted. He'd been honest about that from the beginning. He didn't want commitment—and, as far as he knew, neither did she. It was part of what had made her appealing to him in the first place. He'd told her as much that long-ago night in Los Angeles, he'd repeated it that awful day in Rio...

'Good morning.' Startled, Talia sprang to her feet. Logan smiled at her from the bedroom doorway. 'I thought the smell of coffee might lure you out of hibernation.'

She stared foolishly at the tray and then at him. He looked as if he'd just got out of bed. His hair was mussed and he was wearing only his trousers. Zipped but unfastened, they hung low on his hips. Sunlight dappled his skin with gold and gilded the light covering of hair on his chest and arms. Talia's heart turned over. How beautiful he was. How perfect....

Somehow, she managed a little smile in return. 'Thanks.'

'You're welcome,' he said with teasing solemnity as he set the tray down on the bureau. He leaned back against the door-jamb, his hands tucked into his pockets, and looked at her. 'Coffee first?' A quick smile played across his mouth. 'Or shall we shower?'

It seemed hard to breathe. If he touched her again, if he made love to her, she would be lost. She would say the words she mustn't say, the words she'd almost said last night.

The only safe answer was no answer at all. 'I—I'm sorry I overslept. I must have forgotten to set my alarm. I'll only be a minute.'

'Hey.' He smiled as he came towards her. 'Is that a way to say "good morning"?'

Talia swallowed drily. 'Good morning. Now, if you'd just wait outside while I dress——'

'Talia.' Logan's voice was low. 'Don't be uncomfortable. We're still the same people we were last night.'

Tears stung her eyes with a terrible swiftness, and she blinked them back. She knew he'd meant the words to soothe what he thought was embarrassment. But there was another message in them, as well, although he couldn't know it.

They were exactly the same people they'd been last night. Logan still wanted her in his bed. And she—she wanted him. But she knew she had to have his love, too.

There was only one answer. What had happened between them must not happen again. She would be leaving in just a few days. All she had to do was tell him that last night had been a mistake.

She drew a breath, then expelled it. 'I—I'm afraid I'm not very good at this,' she said with artificial brightness. 'The morning after thing, I mean. I've never quite mastered it. But I wanted to talk to you about—about what happened.'

'Have you had much practice?'

'Much...?'

His mouth twisted. 'The morning after thing.'

'Well, I—I...' Her smile trembled, then faded. 'No. Not—not much.' Not any. She had never spent the night with Keith, she'd never wanted to hold him to her heart...

He smiled. 'Let me teach you, then,' he said, cupping her shoulders in his hands. His eyes darkened as he drew her to him. 'This is how you say "good morning".'

Before she could protest, his mouth took hers in a long, gentle kiss she was powerless to resist.

'How did you sleep?' he asked when he finally let her go.

'I slept—I slept well.'

He smiled. 'So did I. In fact, I had the best night's rest I've had in months.'

'Logan. Please. We have to talk about—about...'

To her surprise, he nodded. 'Yes. You're right, we do. But first we'll have coffee. And then...' His eyes fell to her mouth, then to the curve of her breasts. 'On second thought,' he said thickly, 'perhaps we'll leave the coffee to cool.'

'No.' Her voice was sharp and she swallowed hard before she spoke again. 'I—I'm late enough as it is. I have—I have appointments...'

Her breath caught as his hands slid inside her robe and cupped her breasts. 'Talia,' he whispered, bending to her and kissing her throat. 'Sweet Talia.'

Desire and bittersweet sorrow pierced her heart and raced through her blood, travelling through her body with each swift pulse-beat.

'Put your arms around me, Talia.' His hands slid to her back, warm against her cool skin, and he drew her to him. 'Tell me what I want to hear.'

She knew what he was waiting for her to say. He wanted to hear the admission he'd wrung from her last night, he wanted her to beg him to make love to her. It was what she longed for, too. She ached for his kisses, for the sweet dominance of his body. But there was something she wanted even more, something he wasn't prepared to give.

Tears rose in her eyes and she blinked them away. 'Not—not now,' she said, twisting out of his embrace. 'I told you, I have loads of work waiting on my desk. A report. An important one. John's expecting it. You—you wouldn't expect me to let something like that wait, would you?'

He stared at her in silence, his eyes dark and unreadable, and then he let go of her. 'No,' he said tonelessly. 'I wouldn't. Go on, then. Have your shower. I'll take the coffee downstairs and we can have a cup together when you're ready.'

She let out her breath. 'Yes. That's fine. I—I have some things to ask you anyway, about—about that luncheon you're holding tomorrow.'

His face lost all expression. 'A business breakfast,' he said softly. 'We can get a head start on the day.'

'Yes,' she said quickly. 'Exactly.'

The smile that flickered across his face was an enigma. 'I would never have thought of that,' he said, turning from her. 'I'll see you in a little while.'

Her polite smile collapsed as the door closed after him. She sank to the edge of the bed. How simple it had been to divert his thoughts from her to business. But then, she'd known it would be. Logan Miller had a single-minded dedication to his work.

She had been like that. She had planned her future with care. She had examined every step before she took it. How had this happened to her? If only she were leaving Brazil tomorrow instead of next week. If only...

A muffled sob burst from her throat and Talia buried her face in her hands. She could leave Brazil, but Logan would live forever in her empty heart.

She came down the stairs a short time later, looking cool and composed. Logan was seated at the table near the window; he glanced up when he heard the light tap of her heels.

'Ready for business, as usual,' he said, getting to his feet.

'Of course,' she said calmly, controlling the tremor of her lips. Her glance moved over him. The sexy, half-nude male who'd been ready to make love to her a little while ago had been replaced by a man impeccably attired in a charcoal-grey suit, combed cotton shirt, and tie. 'You, too, I see.'

His lips drew back from his teeth as he pulled a chair out for her. 'I have a full schedule ahead of me today.'

She watched him as he poured her coffee. 'Logan.' He looked up, and she drew a breath. 'About—about last night...'

His laughter was sharp-edged. 'You're going to tell me it was all a mistake.'

Two spots of colour rose to her cheeks. 'Yes. I mean——'

'Don't.' His voice was harsh. 'Lying doesn't become you.' A cold smile tilted the corners of his mouth. 'You can't lie about sex, Talia. A perceptive man knows the truth.'

Sex. She knew that was how he thought of it—it came as no surprise. But it hurt. It hurt...

'It—it was pleasant,' she said, forcing herself to meet his eyes. 'But—but it mustn't happen again.'

Logan's eyebrows rose. 'Mustn't it?'

'No.' If only he wouldn't look at her that way, she thought, as if she were a laboratory specimen under a lens.

'Why not?'

'What do you mean, why not? Surely you can understand——'

'No one need know about us, Talia. We have all the privacy we need up here.'

Colour rose to her cheeks. 'I'd never indulge in a—a sordid little affair, Logan. If I wanted to—to become involved with you, I wouldn't be ashamed of it.'

He smiled. 'Good. That simplifies things, then.'

'Simplifies things?' Talia shook her head. 'What do you mean?'

Logan pushed up his sleeve, looked at his watch, and frowned. 'I'm late for a meeting.' His chair squealed in protest as he shoved it back from the table. 'Can you be here at six?'

She looked at him. 'Yes,' she said slowly, 'I suppose I can. But——'

'I'll see you tonight, then.' He started towards her and she thought he was going to kiss her goodbye. Instead, he touched his hand lightly to her cheek. 'Have a good day,' he said casually, the way sales assistants did when you made a purchase.

Talia watched him as he walked to the lift. He stepped inside, punched in the floor number, and the doors slid shut.

Her heart ached. Logan had never once looked back.

The day moved more quickly than she'd hoped. Bianca greeted her with a problem that needed hours to solve. When she finished with it, it was lunchtime.

She hesitated at the door to the dining-room. Logan had scheduled a luncheon staff meeting for today, with specific orders that she attend. She dreaded what might happen: a proprietorial glance from him, an unexpected meeting of their eyes...

'Talia.'

The sound of his voice startled her. She looked up and watched as he strode down the hall towards her, a gaggle of executives at his heels.

'Hello,' she said. 'I was just—I was just...'

His smile was impersonal. 'Jerry's just told me he's gone on a salt-free diet. See to it that the chef prepares something for him, please.'

She nodded. 'All right.'

'And try not to take too long, will you?' He frowned. 'I want to get this meeting started promptly.'

So much for dreading special treatment, Talia thought, and she nodded again. 'I'll be as quick as I can.' Her voice was as crisp as his.

'Do that,' Logan said, and then turned to the little group behind him, a gesture that made her dismissal clear.

He barely spoke to her during lunch, except to issue an order about a dinner meeting to be held the following week.

'I'll pass it along to Bianca,' Talia said, scribbling a note in her memo book. 'She can tell my successor and——'

Logan's head rose and his eyes met hers for the first time. 'I'll want you to handle this yourself,' he said pleasantly.

'Perhaps you've forgotten. I won't be here then. I'm leaving on the——'

'Didn't I tell you?' His tone was casual, but there was something shark-like in his smile. 'I spoke with John Diamond, and we agreed that the programme's too new to let anyone else handle it. You'll be staying on.'

Talia felt as if the air were being sucked out of her lungs. Easy, she told herself, there's a table filled with people here; if you say the wrong thing or look the wrong way, there's no telling what Logan will do. 'We had a three-month trial agreement, remember?' she said finally, clasping her hands in her lap to keep them from shaking.

He waved his hand. 'My attorney assures me that such a personal services agreement within the contract isn't binding. My deal with Diamond—which includes your participation—is for a full year.' His lips drew back from his teeth. 'I'm afraid you're going to have to withstand the rigours of Brazil a little longer, Talia.' He laughed, and she wondered if she was the only one who heard the falsity in it. 'I must say, you're the only one of my people who's complained about the climate. Isn't that right, gentlemen?'

There was a murmur of agreeable laughter around the table. Talia forced herself to smile along with the others. So, she thought, that was the story he'd told. Well, it wouldn't work. And she doubted if what he'd said about the contract was true. At the next staff meeting, he could damned well try explaining why she'd gone back to the States despite his neat little speech.

She spent the rest of the day in quiet anger, and she welcomed the feeling. It was better than the despair with which she'd begun it. At least anger was an emotion you could do something with. When the lift doors slid open at six that evening, she was spoiling for a confrontation.

Logan was waiting for her with a smile and a glass filled with sparkling, pale golden wine.

'Hello.' He held the glass out to her. 'You're five minutes late.'

'I had a lot to do this afternoon,' she said coolly. 'And I don't want anything to drink.'

His smile broadened. 'This isn't "anything", it's vintage champagne. Go on, take it.'

She took the glass from him reluctantly. There really wasn't much choice: Logan effectively blocked her way.

He lifted his glass to hers. 'Cheers.'

Talia hesitated, then sighed. 'Cheers,' she said, taking a sip.

'Good?'

It was. The champagne was cool and dry. Denying it would be pointless. 'Good,' she admitted, giving him a grudging smile over the rim of her glass.

They had played this scene before, she thought suddenly, the time Logan had met her at the lift with a glass of *caipirinha*. But things were different then. He hadn't made love to her, he hadn't held her all through the night...

She tore her eyes from him and swept past him into the living-room. 'That was a nice bit of nonsense you tried at lunch,' she said, putting her glass down on the coffee-table. 'But it won't work. I'm leaving next week, Logan, and you can't stop me.'

He smiled lazily and leaned back against the wall. 'Can't I?'

There was a huskiness in his voice that made her pulse race. Somehow, he'd made the simple question into a challenge. She knew he might be able to damage her career. But her career wasn't half as fragile as her heart.

Talia's chin lifted. 'Last night didn't change anything. I still intend to return to the States. In fact...' She fell silent. Logan was coming slowly towards her, his eyes dark, his face tense. 'Logan. What are you——?'

'You're going to have to learn to do things properly,' he said softly. He put down his glass, then stopped beside her, so close that, if she lifted her hand, she could touch him. 'There's a way to say "good morning" and a way to say "good evening", and you don't seem to know either.'

Her mouth went dry. 'Don't.'

He smiled crookedly as he bent to her. 'Don't what?' he whispered. His lips brushed her temple, her cheek, touched her ear. She felt the heat of his breath, then the touch of his tongue. A tremor went through her.

'Don't—don't do that. I can't—I can't concentrate when you...' She moaned softly as he lifted the hair from her neck and pressed his mouth to her skin. 'Logan. Please. Please...'

He moved behind her; she heard the rasp of her zip as he drew it slowly open the length of her silk dress. His lips moved against the nape of her neck, his hands slid into the gaping dress and cupped her breasts.

'Oh, God.'

A dizzying sweep of sensation flamed through her. This wasn't fair. Logan was—he was...

Her dress fell away, a silken puddle lying softly at her feet.

'You're so beautiful, Talia,' he whispered.

She wanted to turn in his arms and demand that he stop. She wanted to push free of his embrace and tell him that this meant nothing to her. But she couldn't.

She couldn't. His hands were everywhere, touching, teasing, adding to last night's mysteries.

Logan groaned and drew her back against him.

Her lashes fell to her cheeks as she felt the aroused press of his body. He wanted her—not forever, but for now. And she wanted him. Oh, yes, she wanted him. His kisses, his caresses, his love...

He turned her to him and looked into her eyes. 'I told you that you couldn't lie about wanting this,' he whispered.

Desperately, she cast about for something—anything—that would stop him. 'What about—what about Vitoria Branco?'

His teeth glinted in a feral smile. 'To hell with Vitoria Branco.'

'But I thought—I thought you and she——'

'You thought wrong.' His mouth dropped to hers in a long, hard kiss. When he raised his head, his eyes gleamed with a dark fire. 'You're not leaving Sao Paulo,' he said.

Talia shook her head. 'I must.'

'Damn you,' he growled. His hands tightened on her as he bent and kissed her. His mouth bruised hers; when he looked at her again, she was shaking. 'You're not leaving,' he said again. 'I need you.'

For a breathless moment, her heart soared. He wanted her; he was asking her to stay with him. He was asking her to—to...

'There won't be any strings attached, if that's what's worrying you.' His voice was hoarse, almost angry. 'That's how we'd both want it, wouldn't we?'

Her throat constricted. How foolish to have let herself think he'd ever want anything else. 'Yes,' she whispered, 'that's how we'd want it.'

'That's how it will be, then. An understanding between consenting adults.'

'No. I didn't say that, Logan. I...'

He swept her into his arms and strode through the apartment to his bedroom. Gently, he lowered her to the bed and came down beside her, watching her through hooded eyes as his hand moved over her.

'It's what you want, isn't it?'

When she didn't answer, he kissed her. Slowly, she lifted her arms and wound them around his neck.

A long time later, when they finally lay sated in each other's arms, Logan's heart was racing as violently as hers. He raised himself up on one elbow and looked down at her in the pale light that drifted in from the quiet, night-time city.

'I'll have your things moved down to my rooms in the morning,' he said softly.

Talia's lashes fell to her cheeks. 'Yes,' she whispered. With that one word, she knew she was doomed.

CHAPTER NINE

'TALIA?' Bianca knocked lightly at the half-open office door and stepped inside. She smiled when Talia looked up from the papers on her desk. 'I just wanted to tell you I'm leaving.'

'Goodnight, then. I'll see you in the morning.'

Bianca hesitated. 'It's late, you know. Everyone else has gone. I can stay and help you with those reports, if you like.'

Talia smiled. 'Thanks, but it's not necessary. Besides, it's been a long day. Go on home.'

'Longer for you than for me. Must your Mr Diamond have so many reports each week?'

Talia sighed wearily. 'He says it's the price of success—half a dozen companies have expressed interest since we instituted our programme for Miller International.'

'Here in Brazil, you mean?'

'And in other places. Apparently there are lots of American firms that think John's on to something clever. He's working up a set of fact sheets and a brochure, and he needs all the information I can send him.'

'*Sim*, I understand. But you look——'

'Tired. I know that—you've told me often enough.' Talia's voice had sharpened, and she paused and drew a careful breath. 'Stop worrying about me,' she said, more gently. 'I'm almost finished. Really. I'm going to wrap things up in just a few minutes.'

Her assistant nodded. 'Good. Senhor Miller has already left for the day. He must be wondering what is keeping you.'

Talia's head rose sharply, but Bianca's face was a study in innocence. After a moment, she smiled through stiff lips. 'Don't worry about it,' she said. 'I doubt he's even noticed.'

The young woman nodded. 'As you say. Well, then, *boa noite.*'

'Goodnight. Oh, Bianca—close the door after you, would you, please?'

Talia's smile faded as soon as the door had shut. Her facial muscles felt as tense from holding the artificial smile as did her neck and shoulders from the hours she'd spent at her desk.

She'd have to stop bristling every time her assistant seemed to hint that she knew that Talia's relationship with Logan had changed. Hadn't she told him, after the first time he'd made love to her, that she wouldn't try to hide an affair if they had one? Her words had been brash but safe. One night didn't constitute an affair. Logan had seduced her, and she hadn't been about to let it happen again.

Now, weeks later, those words had a hollow ring. Talia sighed, got to her feet, and walked across her office. It wasn't that she was ashamed of living with Logan. It was just that this was South America and women were not judged by the same standards of morality as men, and . . .

No. That wasn't it at all. She and Logan moved in a sophisticated circle of people who were no different from the ones she'd known back home. Besides, she was a grown woman. Her thirtieth birthday was staring her in the face; how she lived her life was no one's business. Anyway, Logan and she had both been discreet.

A rueful smile touched her lips as she unscrewed the top from a vacuum flask of hours-old coffee. It wasn't as if they were moonstruck lovers. The only visible change between them was the way he behaved when she hostessed the occasional business dinner in his apartment. He seemed to touch her more often than in the past. There was nothing intimate about it—his hand would fall on her shoulder or curve lightly around her waist as they greeted his guests or bade them goodnight.

But there was something proprietorial in the gesture. She could see it reflected in the changed way his colleagues looked at her, and she had yet to decide if it pleased or disturbed her to see the sudden awareness in their eyes.

Talia grimaced as she poured the coffee. The black liquid was oily, almost thick on her tongue, but she held her breath and swallowed it. She needed something to keep her going. Hours of work lay ahead of her—much more than she'd admitted to Bianca—and she was tired, although she suspected that her weariness was as much of the spirit as of the body.

No strings attached. That was what Logan had said, and her reply had marked her agreement. And that was the heart of the trouble. She wasn't ashamed of her relationship with Logan—she was heartbroken by it. Being his lover wasn't enough. What she wanted was to be his beloved. And that was impossible.

She sighed and sank into her chair again. It was probably a good thing they spent so little time alone. Otherwise, who knew what foolish thing she might blurt out? But they were out every evening—dining, dancing, or at the theatre. Logan kept up the pace he'd been accustomed to before they'd become lovers.

Talia had been a little disappointed at first, but then she'd realised that it had been silly to think he'd change, just because of her. Clearly, he was a man who liked going out. Long, lazy evenings at home weren't his style. Which was just as well. There was little time to talk—really talk—at the theatre or the cinema or even in a chic restaurant.

'Did you see this bit about the drought affecting coffee prices?' he'd say.

Or, 'Have you read the reviews of the new James Brooks film? I thought we'd see it this evening.'

Sometimes, as they exchanged polite, meaningless chatter, Talia felt as if she were two people, one the woman who sat opposite Logan, paying polite attention to what he said about explorations for manganese in Minas Gerais or the prowess of a concert pianist, and the other someone who longed to silence him with a kiss, then ask him to tell her things he'd never told anyone else.

'What were you like when you were little?' she wanted to say. 'Did you cry when Bambi's mother was shot? Did you laugh when Mickey Mouse couldn't sweep all the water down the steps of the sorcerer's castle?'

But she couldn't. Logan had laid the ground rules for their relationship at the start, and everything he'd done since then had only refined them further. Intimacy was for the bedroom. He wanted to know Talia's body, but not her soul.

Sighing, she swallowed the last of the stale coffee, then put down the empty mug and rose from her chair. Slowly, she walked to the window, drew open the narrow-slat blinds, and stared out into the darkening street.

What was it she'd learned in a long-ago biology class? You needed certain basics to survive. Food. Drink. Shelter. And, for most people, sex. Nobody had ever mentioned love. Not in biology. 'Love' wasn't a scientific concept. It wasn't a Logan Miller concept, either. In truth, Talia knew little of it herself. She only knew that she wanted more from this man than he was giving her.

Her eyes filled with sudden tears as she stared into the dark street, remembering a rare evening they'd spent at the apartment. Logan had apologetically explained that he had had some work to do.

'You can call Bianca, if you like,' he'd said, watching her as he spread his papers on the table in the living-room. 'She might like to see a film or——'

'No,' Talia had said quickly, 'I—I'd just as soon stay here.' With you, just sitting quietly beside you, watching you, offering you a cup of tea. She hadn't said that, of course. She'd smiled instead and patted her own briefcase. 'I have some work, too, if it's all right.'

He'd said nothing, his face expressionless, and then he'd nodded. 'Certainly.'

But she hadn't worked. She'd pretended to, but in reality she'd simply sat there, surreptitiously watching him from under her lashes, noticing the tiny lines that fanned out from his eyes, the way he had furrowed his brow and thrust his hand into his hair when something in the report he had been reading had puzzled or dis-pleased him.

She had ached to get up and go to him, to put her cool hands on his forehead and soothe him, to kiss the corners of those weary eyes and tell him she——

'Talia?'

The sound of his voice had made her jump. Logan had been watching her steadily, his mouth narrowed to a hard line.

'Sorry.' She'd cleared her throat. 'I must have been—I was so immersed in my work that I——'

'You weren't working at all.' His voice had been curi-ously flat. 'You were looking at me.'

She'd felt the sudden rise of colour in her face. 'Was I?' Her laugh had sounded forced, even to her ears. 'I—I don't think so. I think I was just staring into space and...'

Why had he been looking at her so strangely? There had been a knotted muscle just beside his mouth, his nostrils had been flared...

'What else could I have been doing?' she had finally managed to say, although it came out a raspy whisper.

Logan's eyes had grown dark. They'd locked with hers until she could hardly breathe and then, at last, he'd given a tight little laugh and looked away. 'Nothing else,' he'd said. 'Absolutely nothing else.'

With that, he'd risen from the table and swept his papers together. 'I'm afraid I can't concentrate in this light. I'm going to work in the study—if you don't mind.'

Talia's heart had constricted, but her smile had given nothing away. 'No, of course not.' She'd pushed back her chair and risen, too. 'In fact, I think I'll finish up in my rooms.' She'd laughed nervously. 'Well, you know what I mean. The rooms upstairs.'

Logan had nodded. 'Good idea. I'll see you later, then,' he'd said, as if they had been going to meet at the theatre or some other neutral place.

Now, as she stared blindly into the street, Talia's breath quickened. The place they met—every night—was in Logan's bed. There, in his arms, they came together with a passion that made the empty days and evenings almost bearable. When he made love to her, Logan changed into a different man, one who held back nothing. He was generous and giving, tender as often as he was demanding.

Once, when she'd cried out her pleasure, Logan had drawn back and stared into her flushed face. Talia had reached out for him, but he'd caught her wrists.

'It's never been like this for you, has it?' he'd whispered roughly.

How could it have been? she'd thought, looking at him. She had never been in love before; she'd never dreamed that being in a man's arms could be like this.

But she'd known that that wasn't what Logan had wanted to hear, and finally she'd managed a tremulous smile. 'No,' she'd whispered, 'never.'

Their lovemaking was a miracle, one Talia knew better than to question. But it broke her heart to know that this was all she would ever have of Logan, when she wanted so much more.

Talia sighed wearily. It was late. She could see the headlights of the cars beyond on Avenida Paulista as people hurried home from their jobs. What would they all talk about when they got home? she wondered. Mundane things, probably. They'd share bits and pieces of the day; they'd laugh over little jokes; they'd talk about where to take their next holiday and what to do with the dog when they went away.

The thought of discussing such nonsense with Logan would have been laughable if it wasn't so sad. His wife had undoubtedly tried that and look where it had got her, poor soul. Talia could still envisage the sad-eyed woman in the magazine photo, imagine her distress at the failure of her pathetic attempts to domesticate a man who wanted no domestication.

A small chill moved across her flesh and she shuddered. That wasn't so very different from what her mother had tried to do with her father. Well, the circumstances differed—her mother had been seventeen, a child, really, not a sophisticated woman. And her father had been barely older than that, a boy who was eager to taste life.

'I told her he was no good, but she wouldn't listen. She never did—she never looked beyond tomorrow,' Grams had said whenever she'd retold the familiar story. 'All that mattered was that she wanted to be with him.'

Her mother's pregnancy had resulted in marriage. But, months after Talia's birth, her father had walked out on his bride and his baby daughter and had never looked back. His leaving had freed her mother of any pretence of domesticity and she'd died only a couple of years later, the victim of a drunken, high-speed car crash, leaving Talia to be raised in poverty by an embittered woman grown old before her time.

Talia's eyes glistened with unshed tears. You never knew what cards fate might deal. Here she was, someone who'd carefully constructed a life that was the exact opposite of her mother's, only to be brutally reminded that they shared the same blood, no matter what she might do. But that was where the resemblance to the past ended. Her mother had been a fool, first letting herself get trapped by an unwanted pregnancy and then attempting a marriage with no future.

'Talia?'

She spun towards the door. Logan was standing just inside it, watching her.

'Logan.' Her voice was thick; she cleared her throat. 'I—I didn't hear you.'

He came into the office slowly, his eyes riveted to her face. 'I knocked, but there was no answer. I thought ...' He hesitated. 'Are you all right? You look as if you've been crying.'

'Me?' She laughed as she rummaged in her desk for a tissue. She wiped her eyes, blew her nose, and smiled brightly at him. 'Of course not. I—I think I have some kind of allergy. I couldn't stop sneezing all day.'

'And you look tired,' he said, as if she hadn't spoken. 'Are you sure——'

'I'm fine. I told you, I've been sneezing like mad. And I had a lot of work to get out. John called, and he asked me to ...' She fell silent. Why was he watching her that way? 'Did you—did you want something, Logan?'

He shook his head. 'Not really. I just came to tell you the power's gone off upstairs. The janitor says he doesn't know how long it will take to fix. There's some kind of problem with the line.' He paused. 'Anyway, the fridge is out, of course, and the stove. So I thought I'd go out for dinner.'

'I see.' Talia forced a smile to her lips. 'Well, don't worry about me. I'll finish here and then make myself a sandwich or something. There are candles upstairs, aren't there? I can——'

His eyebrows rose. 'I meant the both of us, naturally. I thought we'd try that new club that opened last week. How does that sound?'

A new club. That meant hordes of people, bright conversation, loud music and louder laughter. Suddenly, the thought of another artificially cheerful evening out was too much. 'You go on without me. I'll finish this report, and then——'

The office lights blinked, then went out, plunging them into darkness. Logan cursed softly.

'Well, that does it.' His voice roughened with impatience. 'Lord knows when the power will come back on now.'

'I have matches some place. Give me a minute to... Here they are. Let me just...'

The match flared in the darkness, burning like a tiny beacon. Logan had already paced to the window. He swore again, then turned towards her. 'The whole damned area's gone out. Who the hell knows how long——?' Their eyes met. In the glow of the flame, his turned from green to burnished gold, like the eyes of a cat.

Talia's heart turned over. 'I—I'll have to find a way to get my work done,' she said. 'Candles, or a torch, or...'

The match fizzled and burned out. Logan shifted his weight; in the darkness, she thought she could hear the sound of his breathing.

'I've nothing but tapers in the apartment.' His voice was low. For some reason, the sound of it sent a tremor through her. 'And there's no way to rig a torch for a reading lamp.' He moved closer to her. In the shadowy darkness, she could just make out his features.

She swallowed drily. 'Then what——?'

'We'll have dinner and wait it out.' Logan's teeth glinted in a quick smile. 'I'm afraid we'll have to try the new club another time, though. It seems as though the street-lamps and traffic lights are out, too. But there must be some place nearby.'

They found a little café two blocks away. Hastily lit candles stood on the tables and threw wavering shadows on the walls. They slipped into a booth and sat facing each other. Usually, Logan began talking about his day or asking about hers as soon as Talia stepped out of the lift at night. Now, silence stretched between them.

After a few moments, a waiter appeared. There was a rapid exchange of Portuguese, punctuated by Logan's laughter, and then they were alone again.

Talia cleared her throat. 'What was that all about?'

Logan smiled. 'He said we could have a menu, if we insisted, but since we wouldn't be able to read it and the cook wouldn't be able to cook, it didn't make much sense to bother. So I told him that was reasonable, and he could bring us whatever he thought we'd like.' His smile broadened. 'He said that was what he'd planned on doing in the first place, and he was pleased to see we agreed.'

Talia laughed. 'Well, it should be an interesting meal, anyway.'

'Yes.' Logan looked around him. 'I've never been in here before.' He smiled at her. 'We'll have to come back when the lights are on and see what it looks like.'

'Probably not half as nice as it does now,' she said, smiling in return. 'I remember once, when I was little...' Her voice faded.

'Go on. What were you going to say?'

Talia shrugged her shoulders. 'It's nothing. I was just remembering one evening when a big storm hit town. Grams had insisted on giving me a birthday party, even though——'

'Grams? Your grandmother?'

She nodded. 'Yes. She raised me. She——' She stopped and looked at him. 'Look, you don't want to...'

Logan reached across the table and put his hand lightly on hers. His touch seemed to sing through her skin. 'What happened to your parents?'

Talia ran her tongue lightly over her lips. 'My father... My father left us when I was a baby. My mother and he... They married too young. She was only in high school...' Her eyes met his. 'She got pregnant,' she said flatly. 'They had to get married.'

'For the sake of the child.' Logan's voice was as flat as hers. 'But it didn't work out.'

'No. They—they weren't happy. Not with each other, not with me.'

She fell silent and his hand tightened on hers. 'You were going to tell me about your birthday party,' he said gently.

She smiled gratefully. 'Right.' She drew a breath, then expelled it. 'I didn't want Grams to arrange one for me. I was ten years old and shy, and...'

His fingers laced through hers. 'I thought you'd have been. Shy, I mean.'

'But there was no talking her out of it. I'd never had a party, you see, because she was always working, and——'

'Never?'

Talia sighed. 'If you want to hear this story, you're going to have to stop interrupting.'

He grinned. 'My lips are sealed.'

'Well, Grams went ahead with her plans. She invited some kids I went to school with, and there we were, gathered around the table and she brought out the cake.' Talia began to smile. 'I was worried about blowing out the candles. Too much breath, and I was sure I'd spit on the frosting. Too little, and the candles wouldn't go out. Either way, I was sure Grams would say something or the kids would laugh—it was bound to be a disaster.'

'And what happened?'

'Nothing, at first. I mean, I barely started—and all the candles went out. Not just the candles. The lights, too. In the house and on the street. Everybody started to laugh. They said I'd blown out the whole town.'

Logan burst out laughing. 'Don't tell me. There was a power failure, and you got blamed for it.'

She chuckled softly and put her hand to her face. 'Yes. Even months later, kids would point at me and say I didn't know my own strength.'

Logan let go of her hand as the waiter put their dinner on the table. He looked down at his plate, then at Talia. 'Any guesses?' he asked.

She smiled. 'Something with lots of spices, from the smell of it. I'll bet it's good.'

He picked up his fork. 'Well, there's only one way to find out. Go on,' he ordered, 'start eating. You not only look tired, you look as if you've lost weight.' A smile spread over his mouth. 'I wouldn't want John Diamond to accuse me of working you too hard.'

Talia smiled in return and picked up her fork. The food was good; it tasted as spicy as it smelled. But she couldn't eat—she was too excited. Carefully, trying not to let him see her do it, she looked at Logan from beneath her lashes. He was so different tonight. It was as if the blackout had plunged them not into darkness but into a different universe.

In all the weeks they'd been together, she had never told him as much about herself as she had in the past few minutes. It surprised her that she'd talked about her parents. She never did, not to anyone. There was no sense to it, it was all in the past and, anyway, it was too personal. As for the story about the candles—it was funny, yes, but it was also terribly revealing. Besides, it was a silly tale. Who'd want to hear it? But Logan had listened with quiet understanding, as if he was really interested. And, at the end, he'd laughed with her, not at her.

'The only power failure I can remember,' he said suddenly, 'was when I was at university. I was in my senior year, and the lights failed the night before final exams.'

Talia looked at him and smiled. 'And everybody sat around praying they wouldn't come on again.'

He laughed. 'Sure. They did, though—just in time for the first exam the next morning.' He pushed aside his plate, put his elbows on the table, and steepled his fingers beneath his chin. 'Were you a good student?' He smiled. 'That's a foolish question, isn't it? I'm sure you must have been.'

Talia moved her plate aside, too. 'I had to be,' she said, almost defensively. 'I was on scholarship. If you didn't do well, you were out.'

He gave her a teasing smile. 'No time to slack off like the rest of us, hmm?'

Her smile matched his. 'Is that your way of telling me you weren't a good student?'

'I refuse to answer that question on the grounds that it may tend to incriminate me.'

She grinned. 'Not fair. You can't quote the United States Constitution to protect your academic record.'

Logan gave her a disdainful look. 'You can if you studied law. Then it's known as utilising your area of discipline.'

'Law? You mean you're an attorney? But I thought——'

'An almost attorney. I never took my bar exams.' He shrugged his shoulders. 'I wasn't serious about the law. I just drifted into it.'

'No one "drifts" into law, Logan. It takes years of study and——'

'Maybe that's the wrong way to phrase it. I just wanted to be anything my father wasn't. He was in business, so I was determined to be in something else.' He smiled. 'I had no talent for music or the arts, and medicine was out because I hated chemistry.'

Talia laughed. 'All of which are excellent reasons for choosing law.'

He grinned. 'They made sense at the time.'

'And then you went to work for your father when you were twenty-two and changed your mind.'

'In Buenos Aires. Yes, that's right. I'm surprised you remembered.'

A light flush rose to her cheeks. 'I have a good memory,' she said lightly. 'It comes of having had to memorise dozens of recipes in school.'

Logan leaned back and looked at her. 'A scholarship student,' he said, smiling. 'I'm impressed.'

Talia gave a little shrug. 'Don't be. I had no choice. I'd always known I'd have to win a scholarship if I was going to go to school and make something of myself.'

'And that was important to you, even then.'

She looked up, caught by the sudden flatness in his voice. Was he becoming bored by all this inconsequential chatter? But Logan was watching her with an interested smile on his face. After a bit, she nodded. 'Yes. No one in my family ever had. I told you about my mother...' She fell silent, and then she cleared her throat. 'Come on,' she said quickly, 'that's enough about me. Tell me something about yourself.'

Logan smiled. 'I have. I just told you all about the backwards way I almost chose a career. What more is there to know?'

Her eyes met his. Everything, she wanted to say, I want to know all there is to know about you, Logan, I want to hear all the details of your life... Instead, she gave him a quick smile. 'Let's see,' she said, wrinkling her brow and pretending deep thought. 'Well, for openers—why didn't you like chemistry?'

'Why didn't I...?' Logan grinned. 'Who knows? Too much math, perhaps.'

Talia shook her head. 'No good. I've seen you tally columns of numbers in a flash, remember? And I know you can figure ratios and percentages without even breathing hard.' She leaned her elbows on the table and propped her chin on her hands. 'Tell the truth, Logan. What's the real reason?'

'The real reason?' His smile grew a little strained. 'You'd laugh if I told you.'

Their eyes met. 'Try me,' she said softly.

Logan inhaled, then let out his breath. 'It's not really much of a story. I was, I don't know, eight or nine, and I had a dog.' He gave a little laugh. 'He wasn't actually mine, he just wandered into our lives one day when I was a toddler.' He smiled. 'God, I loved that dog! He was a big brute of a thing—a Newfoundland.' He leaned across the table, his face alight. 'Do you know the breed?'

She shook her head. 'No. I don't think so.'

'He was huge—he looked like a bear. And he was as devoted as...' He fell silent, then shrugged his shoulders. 'Anyway, he grew old, got a bit smelly and raggedy-looking, but he wasn't ill or anything. My mother had never liked him to start with; she always thought anything bigger than a toy poodle was an embarrassment. And my father was into horses by then; he'd joined a club and its members all fancied themselves as got up in tweed and leather and... Anyway, one day, when I awoke, the dog was gone.'

'Gone? You mean, he'd run off?'

Logan shook his head. 'No.' His voice flattened. 'He was dead. My mother and father had had the chauffeur take him to the vet. He'd been put down.' His eyes, cold as the sea, met hers. 'It was the chauffeur who told me. My mother was too busy—she had a bridge group or the Ladies' League coming to tea, something like that. My father had gone off to his office, so it fell to Charles to be the one to...' He drew a breath. 'I suppose I cried

a lot. That night, my father came to my room. I remember my surprise—he never did that. He'd brought
me a gift. A chemistry set, all shiny and new and, I'm
sure, very, very expensive.' His eyes met hers again, and
the dark rage in them chilled her. 'It was a trade-off,
you see—the set for the dog, as if all those test-tubes
and powders could ever replace...'

For the first time, it was Talia who reached out and
put her hand on Logan's. 'I'm so sorry,' she said softly.

He sat silent for a moment, his eyes averted. She could
feel the tension in him, the tightly strung nerves and
muscles bunched beneath her fingers, and then he pulled
his hand free of hers and looked at her. 'Forgive me,
Talia.' His smile was as strained as his voice. 'I don't
usually go in for self-pity.'

'You have nothing to apologise for. That's an awful
story. How could your parents have been so thoughtless?'

He shrugged his shoulders. 'They weren't thoughtless,
they were simply involved in their own lives. My mother
had her friends and her clubs, my father had his
business.'

'And it was more important to him than anything else.'

Logan looked at her. 'Yes. I didn't understand it then.'
His mouth twisted. 'But I was only a child.'

She hesitated. 'Meaning you—you understand now.'

'Of course,' he said, as if anyone who didn't was a
fool.

Talia smiled sadly. Well, what had she expected? This
night was different from any they'd shared yet, and
Logan had told her a terrible story about a hurt little
boy and a pair of coldly unfeeling adults, but when you
came down to it, nothing had changed. He had left that
little boy far behind; he'd grown into a man like his
father, which wasn't so surprising when she realised how
neatly and easily she'd suddenly followed in her mother's
footsteps.

Logan wasn't about to decide that what he really wanted was a cottage in the country, a dog to replace the one he'd lost as boy, and her beside him forever. She didn't want those things either. She never had. Just because she'd fallen in love with him it didn't mean...

Her heart twisted with sudden anguish. That was exactly what it meant. She wanted Logan forever, she wanted all those commonplace things other people wanted, babies and a tumble of dogs and cats underfoot, she wanted a life she'd never even contemplated...

A life she could never have with Logan.

She sat, stunned and breathless, trying to absorb the impact of the terrible revelation. How could this have happened? She, who had planned things so carefully, she, who had charted her future with such cool precision——

With startling abruptness, the lights blazed to life. People all around them murmured with surprise; some patrons laughed and clapped their hands in appreciation.

Talia and Logan stared across the table at each other. After a moment, Talia stirred uneasily. 'Well,' she said slowly, 'that didn't take very long, did it?'

'No. Not very.' Logan looked around and smiled drily. 'Everything's back to normal again.'

Talia's gaze followed his. In the harsh glare of artificial light, the café stood revealed not as a romantic little cave but as a dingy bistro. She looked at Logan, not trusting herself to say anything, waiting for him to speak instead. Finally, he cleared his throat.

'Talia. About that work you had to do tonight.' He hesitated, and she could see the sudden wariness in his eyes. 'I had some work to do, too, before the lights went out. Now that they're on again, I was wondering...'

Her heart plummeted. Quickly, before he could see the tell-tale shine of her tears, Talia slid from the booth. 'Of course,' she said briskly. 'Let's go. I'd never forgive myself if I don't get that report out first thing in the morning.'

There was a silence, and then Logan rose. 'Fine.' He sounded as he always did, courteous, pleasant—and a little removed. 'Tell you what—why don't you see if you can find us a taxi while I settle the bill? Walking back will only waste time.'

Talia nodded and turned away. It was not only the lights that were back to normal, she thought. Her relationship with Logan was, too. A sorrow greater than any she'd ever known welled within her. So much for magic, she thought, as she hurried out into the night.

CHAPTER TEN

TALIA peered into oncoming traffic, then stood on tiptoe and waved wildly as she spotted a taxi. But her hand fell to her side as it approached—the cab was already taken, just like all the others she'd spotted.

She glanced at her watch, took a deep breath, and began walking quickly along the pavement. She was so late: it was going on seven, which meant that Logan was probably at the apartment by now. What she'd wanted was to be wearing something soft and sexy when he arrived, to hold out a *caipirinha* as the doors to the lift opened and he stepped out...

Instead, she was halfway across Sao Paulo, caught in traffic as heavy as any she'd ever seen. And, as if that weren't enough, she felt sick to her stomach. She'd been queasy yesterday morning—this morning, too, come to think of it. And now the sherry she'd just had with Roberto Santos had brought the queasiness back. Her stomach felt as if it were floating somewhere between her throat and her navel.

Saliva filled her mouth and she swallowed carefully. That was what you got for skipping meals, then eating on the run. Bianca had begged her to take the time for a decent lunch. 'Passing up your own meal programme,' she'd teased. 'What must people think?'

But she'd been too busy today. She'd rushed across town to check wholesale prices at a new market, grabbed a sandwich at a *galeto*, then hurried back to the office for a meeting. And in the middle of everything, there'd been this appointment with Santos...

147

Damn! There had to be another taxi coming. Surely one of them would... Yes! There was one coming now, and it was empty. Talia stepped off the kerb again, ignoring the angry blare of horns, and waggled both hands over her head. Brakes squealed as the taxi swerved and pulled towards her. With a groan of thanks, she pulled open the door and got in. In halting but competent Portuguese, she gave the driver the address of the Miller building, then slumped wearily back in the seat.

The taxi inched forward. At this rate, it would take at least an hour to reach the apartment. Walking might be faster—but the butterflies in her stomach urged her to stay put. Talia sighed. The best she could do was hope that Logan was delayed. She might still have time to mix the drinks, turn on the stereo, and slip into something more feminine than the suit she was wearing.

Lord, how she'd missed him! He'd only been gone two days, but it was the first time they'd been apart and it seemed like forever. The trip had come up suddenly— Logan hadn't even mentioned it until he had been ready to leave the night before last.

'Must you go?' she'd blurted before she'd had time to think.

Logan had stared at her. He'd looked as if she'd suddenly spoken in tongues. 'Does it matter?' he'd said.

At least she'd had enough presence to recover quickly. 'There's a staff meeting tomorrow. Have you forgotten?'

He'd turned away and stepped into the lift. 'It can wait,' he'd said, and the doors had slid shut. He hadn't even kissed her goodbye. But then, he hadn't done lots of things lately. There'd been changes, lots of them, since the night of the power blackout. It was as if the evening they'd spent in the little café, which had seemed for a few brief hours to have brought them closer together, had instead pushed them apart.

At first, the changes had been subtle. Logan seemed to be quieter than usual—there were long silences at breakfast and dinner until finally, in desperation, Talia would either babble something about her work or his. Sometimes, she'd look up to find him watching her, his eyes dark.

She told herself she was imagining things. But, after a while, the changes began to multiply. Going out at night had become almost a compulsion. She'd cherished the few times they'd had quiet evenings at the apartment, even though Logan had always retired to his study after dinner and she'd read or listened to music in the rooms that had once been hers. They had been apart, but that was better than being surrounded by strangers. But the worst change had come in the bedroom, the one place in which they'd always come together with a closeness that had made everything else bearable.

It had started one night when they'd come home late from a supper club. The club had had a tiny dance-floor and a band—not that they'd actually danced much. It had been too crowded to do anything but sway to the music. Talia hadn't minded at all; it was an excuse to feel Logan's arms around her, to hold him close to her, something she didn't dare do unless they were making love.

But Logan had grown irritable. 'Dancing's impossible like this,' he'd said, and he'd led her to their table and called for the bill.

When they'd got back to the apartment, Talia had gone into the bedroom while he'd checked for messages on the answering machine. When he'd joined her, she had been standing at the window in the dark, silhouetted by the faint light from the street below. She had been brushing her hair. It was very long now; she had given up all thought of cutting it after Logan had whispered that he loved the feel of it around him. 'Like a silken tent,' he'd said.

She hadn't realised that he was there until she'd suddenly looked up and seen him watching her with a dark, inexplicable expression on his face.

There'd been a silence, and then Logan had turned away. 'I'm afraid I can't come to bed just yet,' he'd said gruffly. 'There was a message on the machine—something's come up. I'll have to do some work tonight.'

Talia had put down the brush. 'That's all right. I—I have some work I can do while you——'

'No.' His voice had been sharp. 'No,' he had repeated, this time giving her a strained smile. 'Just go on to sleep. There's no sense in both of us staying up.'

It had been the first time she had ever gone to Logan's bed without him. Sleep had been impossible: she'd lain there staring at the ceiling, telling herself that she was foolish to feel hurt. She'd known his priorities, she had from the start. It was true, this room was the one place where their relationship had always come first, but something like this was bound to have happened eventually.

When she'd finally heard his footsteps, Talia had closed her eyes, pretending sleep, waiting for the touch of his hand, the brush of his lips... She'd heard the whisper of his clothing and then Logan had slipped quietly under the blanket without touching her. After a long while, she'd known by the sound of his breathing that he had been asleep.

She had felt a terrible emptiness. Throughout their weeks together, he had never let a night pass without, at the least, holding her in his arms and kissing her.

Perhaps he hadn't felt well. Yes, she'd told herself, that was it. She'd ask him in the morning—unless she awoke to his caresses. She did, often. There was a special tenderness to the way he made love to her in the golden glow of the early sun...

But when she'd awakened, Logan had been gone. She'd found him at the breakfast table, calmly sipping his coffee.

'Logan?' He'd looked at her and she'd hesitated. 'Are you—are you all right?'

'Fine.' He'd smiled politely, then glanced at his watch. 'I want to get an early start on things today. I'll see you later.'

Remembering, Talia sighed. There were still nights when they went to bed together, nights when he took her in his arms and made love to her until she thought her heart would burst with joy and love. And there were still mornings when she awoke to find him holding her, kissing her as if he would never stop. Those were the hardest times of all, the times when she longed to whisper, 'I love you,' instead of 'I want you,' to tell Logan that she wanted not just his lovemaking but his love.

The taxi jerked to a stop and she looked up. The driver turned towards her, speaking too quickly for her to understand, gesturing with his hands. Finally, she realised that he was telling her they were only a little way from her destination, that it would be faster if she got out of the cab and walked.

'*Sim. Obrigado.*' Quickly, she fumbled in her shoulderbag, then stuffed some bills into his hand. The stench of exhaust fumes made her gag as she wove her way towards the kerb.

At least she was almost at the apartment. If only she hadn't agreed to meet Roberto Santos for drinks. But he'd been insistent when he'd called, saying he had a business proposition to discuss. Talia had tried to make him understand that she had nothing to do with any part of Logan's business except for the catering end.

'It is you I must see,' he'd said. 'It is important.'

It had all seemed very confused and mysterious, but there had been no way she could reach Logan to ask what she should do. Finally she'd agreed to meet Santos at the Eldorado.

Now, hurrying the last block towards the apartment, Talia shook her head with annoyance. Santos hadn't wanted to talk to Logan at all; what he'd wanted was to try and convince her to leave Miller International and go to work for him, instead.

She pushed open the lobby doors and hurried towards the lift. It had taken time until he'd come out with it. By then, precious minutes had ticked away so that here she was, late when she'd so badly wanted to be early, out of breath and still queasy and...

The lift doors slid open. Talia hesitated, then stepped out. Her heels tapped lightly against the terracotta tiles. Logan was nowhere to be seen. She put her hand to her racing heart. Maybe she'd made it in time. Maybe there was time to take something for her stomach and then chill the wine, although the thought of drinking any made her feel even worse. Maybe...

'I see you finally got here.'

She whirled around. 'Logan. I was just wondering...' Her smile faded. There was such a cold look on his face, it chilled her to the bone. She took a step towards him. 'I—I'm sorry I'm late.'

'You are. Very late. Where were you?'

'I—I was out,' she said. 'Something unexpected came up, and——'

'Something unexpected.' His lips drew back from his teeth in a smile that was not a smile at all. 'And what might that have been?'

She stared at him. 'I was—I was called away on business. Roberto telephoned, and——'

Logan's eyes were cold. 'And it was more important to meet him than to wait here for me.'

Colour rose in her face. 'I told you, I tried to get back on time. And it was important, yes. Roberto said——'

'And, of course, you went.' She nodded. 'Well, what did he want?'

She thought of fabricating a story. Telling Logan the truth might drive a wedge between the two men. But something in Logan's expression warned her not to lie. 'He—he offered me a job. He's opening a restaurant in Rio and——'

His eyes went blank. 'Did you accept?'

Talia stared at him in disbelief. 'How can you ask me that? No, of course I didn't. I——'

'Why not? Isn't the salary high enough?'

She felt herself grow pale. 'Logan. Please, you're not being fair. You know I wouldn't——'

His lips drew back from his teeth. 'No, I don't suppose I am.' There was a pause, and then he turned and walked towards the drinks tray on the far side of the room. 'And forgive me for questioning you. Of course you had to meet with Santos. I understand.'

She took a step towards him. 'You're not angry, then?'

He turned to her and smiled. 'Would you like a drink?'

'Just some mineral water, please.'

He poured her a glass of Evian, then reached for a glass already half-filled with a colourless liquid. He'd been drinking before she arrived, she thought with surprise. As she watched, he topped the glass up, then took a swallow.

'I'm not new to this kind of scene,' he said, walking to the window and staring out. 'I played it often enough with my wife.' He laughed. 'Forgive me. My *ex*-wife.' He tilted the glass to his lips again and drank.

Talia nodded. Of course. She wondered how many times Logan had left his wife to go off on business, how many empty nights the woman had faced.

The ice in his glass tinkled as he tipped it to his mouth. 'Aren't you curious about what happened to my marriage, Talia? Haven't you ever wondered why it failed?'

She swallowed drily. 'I—I didn't think you wanted to talk about it,' she whispered. 'And I know most of what happened. She—your wife—wanted things that you didn't. You . . .'

He grinned, and a chill went through her. He was drunk. Not enough to impair his reactions or slur his speech, but . . .

'That's right,' he said. 'We had very different ideas about marriage. About relationships.' He took a long swallow of his drink, then looked at her over the rim of his glass. 'We talked about it endlessly. But it was pointless. In the end, what she wanted and what I wanted were poles apart.' He eyed his empty glass, then walked to the drinks tray and refilled it to the top. 'By the time we divorced, we were both relieved to have it done with.'

Talia stared at him. He had never spoken so intimately about himself, except for the night in the café. And she had never seen him so out of control. Her heart slammed against her ribs. What was going on?

'All of which,' he said in a slightly slurred voice, 'is a long-winded way of saying no, I'm not angry with you for putting what's important to you ahead of anything else.'

'I told you, I had no choice. Roberto——'

Logan held up his hand. 'No explanation necessary. Hell, one of the reasons I wanted you working for me was because you were such a crack businesswoman.' He smiled. 'What you did was nothing less than I expected.'

Nothing less than he expected. And nothing less than he would do himself. Talia felt the sudden prickle of tears in her eyes, and she blinked them away. Say something, she thought. Say something, don't just let the silence drag on. 'Was it—was it difficult? Your divorce, I mean. I should think it must be—it must be hard to give up someone you—you . . .'

'Care for?' Logan laughed. 'There was no caring left by then, believe me.' He raised his glass and took a sip.

'But it was hard. Sure it was. Saying goodbye is never easy—you always remember the good times, not the bad.' His mouth tightened. 'We even tried a reconciliation. But you can never go back. Once a thing is over, it's over.'

'At least you tried.'

He looked across the room at her. 'It only made it worse,' he said sharply. 'My wife thought she'd become pregnant.' A shadow passed over his face. 'But she wasn't, and once I was certain of that...'

His voice was filled with passionate intensity. Talia stared at him. 'Didn't you want a child?'

Logan looked at her as if she were crazy. 'A child? God, that's the last thing...' His lips compressed into a tight line. 'Everybody has their priorities. You, of all people, should understand that.'

You, of all people... Dear God, what a monster he thought she was! As far as he knew, her career was everything to her. It was why he'd been drawn to her in the first place. And the worst of it was that he had been right. She would have understood it, before she'd fallen in love with him. The terrible obscenity of it all made her throat constrict. Logan had made her aware of a part of herself she'd spent a lifetime denying—and he would never know it.

Nausea rose within her like a sea rising up at the start of a storm. She turned her back, taking deep breaths until the sensation subsided, but even when it had the feeling of illness remained.

He was still talking, but she couldn't listen any more. The things he'd told her were too revealing. His revelations about himself and his failed marriage weren't new—Talia had known most of it from the articles she'd read about him and the things John Diamond had said—but, somehow, hearing them from his own lips made them seem even worse. And knowing that Logan saw

her as a mirror image of himself made the charade she
was living with that much harder to bear.

'Logan.' Talia swallowed. 'I wonder—would you mind
if I lay down for a while? I—I've had a rough day and
I'm a little tired.'

'Of course. Forgive me for going on for so long.' He
looked at her and, for an instant, she thought she saw
pain in his eyes. But then he smiled and turned away,
and she could see only his taut body and tensed
shoulders. 'Why don't you nap upstairs,' he said casually, 'in your old room? That way, I won't disturb you
while I unpack.'

It took all the strength she had not to cry out in pain.
Everything was beginning to add up: his odd behaviour
the past weeks, his coming to bed later and later, his
rising before her in the mornings.

And now she understood why he'd told her all this
about himself. Once a thing is over, it's over. That was
what he'd said and that was his message. He had finished with her, and he was trying to tell her that as kindly
as he could.

Somehow, Talia managed to nod her head. Somehow,
she managed to climb the stairs. She felt as fragile as
crystal as she opened the door and stepped inside. Carefully, she walked into the bedroom—and then, with a
suddenness that almost tore her apart, her stomach rose
into her throat.

She clapped her hands to her mouth and flew into the
bathroom. Doubled over in pain, she retched again and
again, until there was nothing left. She rinsed her mouth,
washed her face, then walked slowly through to the
bedroom and sank down on the bed.

Maybe she had a virus. Maybe she had food poisoning.
Maybe...

Her eyes went to the little calendar she'd left, forgotten, on the bedside table. She stared at it a moment,
then snatched it up. Quickly, she thumbed back a month,

then two... A moan broke from her lips and the calendar slipped from her hand to the floor.

She was her mother's daughter, all right, but she was a far greater fool than her mother had ever been. At least her mother had had some kind of excuse for what had happened to her. She'd been only seventeen—what could she have known of life? Talia was almost thirty. She was a woman—an intelligent, cosmopolitan, well-educated woman.

None of which, she thought as she bowed her head and buried her face in her hands, *none* of which had kept her from becoming pregnant.

CHAPTER ELEVEN

TALIA cried until there were no more tears to shed, and then she dried her eyes and walked slowly to the window. There were no choices, she thought, as she stared blindly into the night. That simplified things, it made what had to be done easier.

She had to leave Brazil, leave Logan, and never look back. It was something she'd always known would happen, ever since he'd set the rules for their affair and she, by her silence, had agreed to abide by them. That she'd fallen in love with him wasn't his responsibility. Nor was her pregnancy.

'I assume you're using protection,' he'd said bluntly, some time during the first few days of their passion.

Talia wasn't. There'd been no reason to worry about birth control, not since those long-ago times with Keith, and he'd taken care of those things, not she. But there was something too revealing about admitting that she wasn't taking the pill, that she had no device of any kind.

'Yes, of course,' she'd said, looking away from him.

That morning, she'd called the American Embassy and asked for the names of English-speaking doctors in Sao Paulo. But she'd waited days for an appointment—and now it was obvious that by the time she'd seen the doctor, it had already been too late.

Now she was pregnant. Just like her mother. And she was carrying the child of a man who wanted no part of her—again, just like her mother.

Tears rose in her eyes and she wiped them away with the back of her hand. That was where the resemblance ended, though. She wasn't the childish fool her mother

158

had been, she wasn't some silly young thing from Hicksville who couldn't think straight.

Quickly, she pulled her clothing from the wardrobe, then from the bureau drawers. She wasn't about to have a child out of wedlock. She wasn't about to have a child at all. It was one thing to be a fool for love. But it took an imbecile to bring an unwanted baby into the world.

When she was packed, she shut off the bedroom light, locked the door, and sat on the bed, in the dark, waiting. Hours passed, and then she heard Logan's footsteps on the stairs. She held her breath while he knocked at the sitting-room door.

'Talia?'

She said nothing when she heard the door open, heard him walk slowly across the room to the bedroom door.

'Talia?' he called softly.

Her heart pounded when the doorknob turned. There was a moment's silence, and then the sound of his retreating footsteps. Talia rose, hurried to the door, and pressed her ear to it. Yes, she could hear the hiss of the lift doors, the hum of the lift as it descended...

Her lip trembled. She'd been right, then. Logan would be out tonight, he'd be picking up his life where it had been left off—probably with Vitoria Branco. A sudden vision of Vitoria and Logan assaulted her senses. She saw the woman leaning over him, her dark hair falling on either side of his rapt face.

Like a silken tent, Talia. Like...

A sob burst from her throat. Quickly, she unlocked the door, opened it, then picked up her suitcase.

She never paused to look back.

It was late the next night when she rang the bell at John Diamond's apartment in San Francisco. The look of astonishment on his face when he saw her brought a smile to her lips for the first time since she'd left Brazil.

'Talia?' he said, staring as if she were a ghost. 'What the hell are you doing here?'

'Hello, John,' she said wearily. 'Do you think you could ask me in before we get to the question and answer period?'

Her boss shook his head. 'Sorry. Yeah, come on in. Would you like something? Coffee? Tea? Something stronger?'

She sighed as she sank into a chair. 'Nothing, thanks.' She smiled again as she looked into his puzzled face. 'You might want something, though. Something stronger.'

Diamond blinked. 'OK, let's have it. What are you doing in San Francisco?'

Talia's smile faded. 'He hasn't—Logan hasn't called, then?'

John had stared at her. 'No. Should he have?'

She sighed again and put her head back against the chair. It was foolish to imagine that he might have, she thought, closing her eyes. Logan must have breathed a sigh of relief when he had found her gone the next morning. It was easier this way. Cleaner. He was a man with no heart, but he'd tried to end their affair with some kindness, first with subtle hints, then more directly when she couldn't—or wouldn't—catch on.

'Talia?'

She blinked. 'Sorry,' she said with a little laugh. 'I— I haven't had much sleep. I feel as if I've been flying for days and days and...' Talia drew a breath. 'I'm not going back to Sao Paulo, John. I'd have given you warning if I could, but...'

John sat down opposite her. 'What's that supposed to mean? You have a job down there, or have you forgotten? Miller won't let you just——'

Her eyes met his. 'Yes, he will,' she said softly.

Diamond stared at her. 'I don't suppose it would do me any good to ask you to explain that.'

'No. It won't.'

He laughed. 'Well, that's direct enough.' He rose, scratched his head, then blew out a breath. 'OK. Can that girl you trained—what's her name?'

'Bianca.'

'Right. Bianca. Can she handle things for a while?'

'Yes, absolutely. In fact, I don't think you need to replace her. She's very capable. Let her hire an assistant, and——'

He held up his hand. 'I'll call her right away.' He waited, then looked at Talia. 'Listen, kid, I'm not asking for details. But you look kinda—I mean, is there anything I can do?'

The unexpected offer, and the sudden gentleness of his voice, startled her. She looked at him and started to speak, when all at once tears filled her eyes. John muttered something as she shook her head and turned away in embarrassment.

'I'm sorry,' she said with an awkward laugh. 'It—it must be jet lag.'

'Listen, maybe you should take a break for a few days. Go up the coast, relax...'

Take a few days... The thought of the ordeal that lay ahead was enough to send a pain knifing through her heart. 'Yes,' she murmured, 'that's a good idea. I—I'll take a week, John. Is that all right?'

Her boss sighed. 'Sure,' he said, slipping an arm around her shoulders. 'No sweat. You just go somewhere nice and have a good time.'

She thought of those words the next day as she sat in her apartment, telephone in hand, working up the courage to call her gynaecologist and—and arrange what had to be done. Have a good time, John had said, have a...

That afternoon, she sat facing her doctor. Yes, she was pregnant. There was no question about it. And, if she wanted an abortion, it had to be done soon.

Talia nodded. 'All right,' she said in a whisper. 'How about—how about the end of next week?'

Why had she said that? It had to be done soon—the sooner the better. There was no point in ... She blinked. The doctor was shaking his head, telling her he would rather make the arrangements for tomorrow.

'No,' she said quickly. He looked at her, and she drew her breath. 'I mean I—I have to decide. I can't just ...'

He smiled gently. 'There's another option, Miss Roberts. Have you considered carrying the child to term and then giving it up for adoption?'

Talia stared at him. 'Give it up? My baby?' She shook her head. 'I couldn't do that. I couldn't give it away and never know ...'

Her words tumbled to a halt. What was she saying? She didn't want this baby. Then what did it matter if she never knew what happened to it? It would be well cared for and loved—wasn't that all that mattered?

Her eyes filled with tears. Oh, God, why was she telling herself all these lies? Of course she wanted her baby. It was already a part of her. And it was Logan's child; it had been conceived in love, even if it had only been her love. She wasn't her mother, she was a grown woman, responsible and capable. She had some savings, she had a way to earn her own living. There would have to be some changes in her life, yes, but she was ready for change. She was more than ready. The past months had taught her that.

'Miss Roberts?'

She looked at her doctor. 'When is my baby due?' she asked, and then she laughed through her tears. 'And what special things should I do to make sure it's healthy?'

Talia went home happy, truly happy, for the first time in weeks. Her head was filled with plans for the future. John would have to agree to giving her a year's sabbatical. After that, she'd work part-time. Her baby would come first, it would give her life the meaning it had for so long lacked. She would give it all the love that had been locked in her heart for so many years.

She had no way of knowing that, in the end, her planning would come to nothing. Only days later, she awoke to a sudden, agonising pain and the sticky warmth of blood on her thighs. Somehow she managed to telephone for help before she collapsed. When she awoke, in a stark white hospital room, she knew what had happened even before she saw the doctor's sympathetic face.

'I'm sorry, Talia,' he said softly.

Her eyes filled with tears. 'Was it—was it because I didn't think I wanted the baby?'

He smiled and shook his head. 'No, of course not. It just happened, that's all. That's how nature is. Sometimes things just happen, and it's past our understanding.'

He said more—that she was still young, that she was healthy, that she could look forward to having lots of babies. But Talia wasn't listening. There would be no babies, not for her. She would never love again. She knew that instinctively, just as she knew she would never get over Logan. In some terrible way, losing his child was almost like losing him all over again.

Set against the rugged slopes of Mount Mansfield, the town of Stowe, Vermont looked like an artist's sketch of a New England village. And on this winter Sunday, with its white-steepled church and clapboard and brick houses cloaked in a fresh fall of snow, the town was a Currier and Ives print come to life.

Standing at the square-paned window of the house she'd bought, looking out at the quiet scene, Talia shivered, then drew her wool shawl more closely around her shoulders.

The temperature was dropping outside. She knew that because the house was getting colder. The heating system was antiquated—she'd known it when she'd bought the

place—and the worsening weather put an almost un-
bearable strain on the old burner's ability to keep up.
The snow was picking up, too. Even the laconic Yankee
natives were beginning to say that this was the harshest
winter to hit the region in years.

Sighing, Talia crossed the wide-planked floor to the
far side of the room, where a fire glowed on a stone
hearth. The logs were burning well, filling the room with
the scents of apple and oak. But she would need more
wood soon—the basket beside the hearth was almost
empty—and if she was going to go outside and bring
some in, the time to do it was now, while there was still
some daylight.

A gust of wind rocked the house, moaning like a wild
thing as it skimmed through the eaves. Quickly, before
she could change her mind, she pulled on her boots,
slipped into a mackinaw and gloves, and opened the back
door.

She shuddered, averting her face as wind-whipped
crystals of snow raked her cheeks. She'd always loved
snow—it was what she'd missed most, years ago when
she'd moved from her native New York State to
California. But she'd been younger then, or perhaps
simply more filled with hope and expectation. Now, the
thick white fall seemed more threatening than beautiful.

She bent carefully, from the knees, trying not to put
too much strain on her back. But it twinged anyway and
she gritted her teeth as she scooped up an armful of logs.
Straightening slowly, she looked into the overcast sky,
then marched back to the house, shouldered open the
door, and deposited the wood beside the fireplace. She
made two more trips outside before her aching back and
arms told her that it was time to stop. With a groan, she
peeled off her outer clothing, kicked off her boots, and
sank to the rug before the hearth.

She wondered, not for the first time, what had possessed her to move to Vermont. It had seemed such a

clever idea, a couple of months ago. She had checked out of the hospital knowing that she could never go back to her old life. Her career, her steady climb to the top, had no meaning any more. She needed time to reassess her values, to reorganise her life. She needed a new beginning.

Vermont had been as far from her old job and her old life as night was from day. It had seemed the right place to start over. Choosing Stowe had been simple. The town had a well-to-do population that swelled its ranks on weekends and holidays. They were people who came to ski and party, weary after the rat-race in the cities. Talia had gambled that they'd be happy to pay the price for her ready-made ragouts, soups, and crusty French breads.

John Diamond had tried to talk her out of it. He'd looked at her as if she were crazy when she'd told him she was leaving the West Coast and striking out on her own. And he'd yelled and cursed a lot—which was no less than she'd expected. Still, in the end John had hugged her, given her a quick kiss, and wished her well.

'Break a leg, kid,' he'd said, and for a moment it had been like the old days.

But only for a moment. Her smile had faded as quickly as it had come, and John had put his arm around her shoulders.

'What is it, Talia? I know there's something wrong. If you want to talk about it . . .'

But she'd shaken her head, not trusting herself to answer. She'd lost everything, Logan and her baby, but she hadn't been about to tell John Diamond that. As far as he knew, she'd simply grown weary of the city and decided to try her own wings.

A piece of wet wood hissed as the flames caught it and a tiny geyser of steam rose towards the flue. Talia sat up, took the poker, and shifted the logs carefully.

Her back twinged again and she bit down on her lower lip. All her muscles were beginning to ache.

She'd have to take things a little easier. Turn the heat up, perhaps, even if it meant feeding more oil to the voracious appetite of the burner. Well, there was some money left in her account. Not much—the down payment on the house had taken almost all her savings, and her living expenses had just about depleted what little remained. But things would pick up soon. It took time to get a new business started, she knew that.

Sighing, Talia closed her eyes and lay her head back against the couch. John had called her the other evening. 'Don't you get lonely up there,' he'd demanded, 'with nothing but cows to keep you company?'

And she'd laughed and said that there were plenty of people in town and, besides, she had her work to keep her busy. But the truth was that she was lonely all the time. Once, she'd thought she heard a baby crying. It was only the wind sighing through the trees, but her eyes had filled with tears at the sound.

She dreamed a lot, too. She dreamed of Logan. But it wasn't the way it had been months before, when they'd first met. Then, she'd dreamed of the magic of being in his arms. Now, she dreamed of a different kind of magic—of the times she'd awakened in his arms with the morning sunlight warm on her face, of the way they'd talked at the little café the night of the blackout, of how they'd laughed together in Rio.

Her hand went to her throat and her fingers closed lightly around the amulet he'd bought her that afternoon. She knew she should have taken the *figa* off long ago and thrown it away, but she could never bring herself to do it.

'Logan,' she whispered. 'Logan.'

Pain closed around her heart, almost crushing it. She sat up quickly, grasped the poker and stabbed blindly at the smouldering logs.

What was the matter with her today? The weather, maybe. It had been overcast for days. Hadn't she read something about a lack of sunlight causing depression? Talia rose quickly and walked to the little office just off the kitchen, switching on the lights and resetting the thermostat as she passed. There had to be some kind of work she could do to busy herself, even if it was only mindless paper-shuffling.

She really did feel awful. She'd begun to get a headache to complement her backache, and she was still chilly, even though this was the warmest room in the house. Maybe she was coming down with something; the man who delivered her wood had mentioned that everybody seemed to have the flu. Actually, she'd been feeling off for days, and she was probably a prime candidate—she'd lost weight and she didn't sleep very well.

She groaned softly as she reached for a bulky sweater and pulled it on. She couldn't afford to be ill—she had her first decent order to fill for the weekend: beef burgundy and chicken chilli, salads and a chocolate mousse for a party. If she was sick . . .

The shrill ring of the telephone made her start. She put her hand to her heart as she hurried across the room and lifted the receiver. Please, she thought, let it be another order, even if it was just for sandwiches.

'Good afternoon.' She winced. Her throat hurt, and she tried clearing it. 'Stowe-It Catering. May I help you?'

John Diamond's groan sounded softly in her ear. 'Stowe-It Catering, huh? That's so cute, it ought to carry a warning.'

Talia sighed and sank into the rocking-chair. 'It's not as bad as some of the other names I've seen. How does The Gay Gourmet strike you?' He groaned again and she laughed. 'How are you, John?'

'I'm fine. But you sound as if you're coming down with something.'

'You're probably right. The flu's making the rounds up here.'

John clucked his tongue. 'That's what you get for living in the boondocks.'

'It's not the boobdocks,' Talia said patiently.

'Yeah, yeah, I know. It's a big ski town, and all the skiers are gonna beat a path to your door and buy your goodies.' There was a pause. 'Are they? Beating a path to your door, I mean.'

The oil burner gurgled, then belched loudly. 'Business is picking up,' she said. 'It's not booming, but——'

'You could always come back to work for me, you know.'

She smiled. 'Thanks, but——'

'But no thanks.' John sighed deeply. 'I just don't understand it, kid. You were on a fast track to the top, and then you just decided to walk away. What happened?'

Talia closed her eyes, then opened them again. 'We've been through this before. I told you, I—I just decided that I needed a change of pace. I'd have thought a veteran of the sixties would understand that.'

'Yeah, well, you're gonna have to get back in the race one last time. I got a letter faxed from Logan Miller the other day.'

Her heart thudded. 'What's it got to do with me?'

She heard the sound of paper crackling. 'Well, let me—yeah, here it is. He says he's been trying to locate you. He says——'

Talia jumped to her feet. 'You must be wrong, John. He wouldn't——'

'Listen, are you reading this or am I? It says right here, "I should very much like to contact Talia Roberts."'

She sank back to the chair, trying to still the crazy leaping of her pulse. 'What else does he say?'

'He says you did a good job in Sao Paulo, blah, blah, blah, that his company's prospering, blah, blah—here we go.' John cleared his throat. '"In fact,"' he read, '"we are about to open an office in Dallas, and we want to recreate the successful meal programme you and Miss Roberts initiated for us ín our Brazil facility. To that end——"'

'John. What has this to do with——?'

'He wants you to act as consultant.'

Talia stared at the phone as if it had metamorphosed into a snake. 'He wants...'

'I phoned and told him you didn't work for me any more. And I said——'

'I hope you said it's out of the question.' Her voice was sharp.

There was a pause. 'I told him I'd check with you, which is what I'm doing. Look, you said yourself that nobody's beating a path to your door, Talia. Hell, you can pick up a bundle.'

'Forget it.'

'Talia.' John's tone softened. 'What would it take? A couple of quick trips to Texas? Hey, most people would pay for the chance to dig out from under a zillion feet of Vermont snow and——'

'Goodbye, John.'

'Look, argue with Miller, not with me. He says you're the only one who can do the job. So I gave him your address——'

She slammed the phone down, then folded her shaking hands in her lap. Easy, she thought, take it easy. It wasn't John's fault. He didn't know anything. Besides, how could she blame him when it was Logan's fingerprints that were all over the story?

Her head spun as she got to her feet. Aspirin. She needed aspirin. And hot tea. Then she'd go to bed and curl up under the duvet.

Miller says you're the only one who can do the job.

It had never occurred to him that she'd turn him down, even though she'd walked out on him and her job in the middle of the night.

A sob broke from her lips and she clapped her hand to her mouth. How ironic that she, who had never *wanted* to love, should have fallen in love with a man who didn't know *how* to love. There was a terrible irony to it, an awful rightness that two such emotional cripples should have——

Something slammed against the door. A branch, she thought, taken down by the wind. She started forward and the room seemed to spin away, then turn grey. She leaned back against the wall, waiting for the world to right itself, and the sound repeated. Was there someone at the door, on a night like this? Surely no one would come out for a take-away meal in the midst of a snowstorm?

The knock came again, impatient and angry. 'All right,' she croaked. 'I'm coming.'

The door swung open. Snow swirled into the room, in a mad dance of icy flakes, and a man stepped through the door. Talia stared at him, at the gold-streaked hair now dusted with snowflakes, at the broad shoulders and lean body...

'Logan?' The word was a papery whisper drawn from her aching throat.

'Yes. You're damned right it's...' He took a step forward. 'Talia? Are you ill?'

'Me?' She leaned away from the wall. 'No,' she said clearly, 'not at all.'

And then her eyes rolled up into her head and she tumbled into his arms.

CHAPTER TWELVE

THE night passed in a blur of half-remembered images and fleeting sensations. Talia felt the brush of cool hands on her fevered skin, heard a husky voice urging her to drink the liquid being spooned between her lips, saw a shadowed face swimming above her. When she awoke the next morning, weak but clear-headed, she thought she must have dreamed it all.

But she had no memory of going to her bedroom and none of undressing. Yet here she was, in bed, in her flannel nightshirt. She struggled to sit up but the effort exhausted her and she sank back against the pillows. Logan, she thought, remembering. But that was impossible. She was ill—she knew that much. If she'd run a high fever, perhaps she'd hallucinated. Perhaps she'd imagined it all.

'Good morning.'

Talia's breath caught. Logan was no hallucination. He was reality, standing in the open doorway, watching her expressionlessly, a glass of orange juice in his hand.

'What—what happened?' she asked. 'What are you doing here? Why...?'

A smile curved across his face. 'How do you feel?'

She swallowed. 'Better than last night. Was I—was I very ill?'

Logan walked to the bed and sat down beside her. 'Here,' he said, holding out the glass of juice, 'drink this. And take this tablet.'

'What is it?'

'It's an antibiotic. The doctor says you're to take them for the next week.'

'The doctor? But——'

'Everything in good time,' he said patiently. 'First the pill and the juice, then I'll get you to the bathroom, and when you're back in bed, we'll talk.'

She felt her cheeks redden. 'I don't need help to the bathroom, thanks. I can manage on my own.'

Logan's eyes became shuttered. 'Yes, I saw how well you managed on your own. You've lost weight and you were walking around with a case of the flu that would have put an ox down.' He put the tablet to her lips. 'Take this and stop arguing.'

Obediently, she opened her mouth and he put the tablet on her tongue. That taste of his skin was shockingly familiar; it sent a sharp wave of bittersweet memory through her.

'Now drink the juice, Talia. All of it, to the bottom. You lost a lot of fluids last night, sweating out that fever.'

The images came again, strong yet gentle hands peeling off her damp nightgown before replacing it with another, those same hands drying her body... Again, colour leaped to her face. 'You—you undressed me.'

Logan gave her a grim smile as he put aside the empty glass, then drew back the blankets and lifted her into his arms. 'That's a charmingly modest reaction,' he said drily as he carried her to the adjoining bathroom. 'But I didn't see anything of you I haven't seen before.' He set her down gently on the floor. 'Now, can you manage on your own? Or shall I stay?'

'I can manage,' Talia said quickly.

'Are you sure? You don't look any too solid to me.'

'I'm positive.' She sighed when she saw the unyielding look on Logan's face. 'I'll be fine,' she said with a quick smile. 'Really.'

He nodded. 'I'll be just outside the door, if you need me.'

Her smile faded as the door swung shut and a sudden wave of weakness made her reach out to the sink and cling to it for support. Logan, here? It was impossible. Why had he come? She thought back to yesterday's call from John Diamond. No, that was insane. Logan had been arrogant enough to expect her to agree to set up a new catering programme for him. But he wouldn't be fool enough to come all the way up here to try and convince her to do it.

Talia sank down on the closed toilet seat. Yes, he would. If Logan Miller wanted something badly enough, nothing would stop him.

'Talia?'

She jumped as he rapped sharply on the door. 'Yes,' she said, 'I'm all right. Just give me another few seconds.'

There was a tray on the night table and he was re-making her bed when she finally emerged from the bathroom and leaned weakly against the jamb. Logan plumped her pillows one last time, then turned towards her.

'Better,' he said, his eyes flicking over her. 'But still not good.'

She flushed beneath his impersonal scrutiny. She'd managed, despite the feeling that her legs didn't quite belong to the rest of her, to wash, brush her teeth, and comb her hair. But make-up had been beyond her, not that she'd have bothered putting any on if she could. Logan was here on business. It didn't matter to him what she looked like, just so long as she agreed to his terms. And she would never do that, no matter how he'd helped her last night. She had agreed to his terms once before, and it had left her with a broken heart.

'I'm not in a beauty pageant,' she said coolly.

His smile was tight. 'I was talking about the state of your health,' he answered. Before she could take another step, his arms closed around her and he lifted her from the floor and crossed the room. 'As for the other...' She heard the sharp rasp of his breath as he lowered her to the bed and drew the blankets over her. 'As for that, you're just as beautiful as ever.'

She looked up at him, stunned as much by the huskiness of his voice as by his words, but he had already turned away. When he looked at her again, his expression was impassive. 'All right,' he said briskly, putting the bed-tray across her lap, 'I want every bit of this eaten.'

Talia looked at the toast and cereal in front of her and paled. 'I don't think I can. I'm not used to eating that much in the morning.'

His mouth narrowed. 'Or any other time of day, from the looks of you.'

'And you said you'd explain things. You said——'

'What I said was, first things first.' He scooped some cereal into the spoon and held it out to her. 'Have your breakfast, and then we'll talk.'

Somehow, she managed to make a respectable dent in the level of the bowl and to eat half the toast. Finally, she groaned and turned her face away.

'Please,' she said, 'not another mouthful, Logan. I won't be responsible for what happens if you make me take another bite.'

He looked at her, sighed, and rose to his feet. 'OK. I'll let you rest for a while. But you'll have to do better at lunch.'

'Wait a minute!' Her cry stopped him as he started out of the room. He stopped and turned to her. 'You said you'd explain after I ate breakfast.'

He smiled pleasantly. 'I lied.' He winked at her, and the door closed softly after him.

Talia lay back against the pillows. She knew she ought to go after him and demand that he answer her questions. But she was exhausted. She sighed and rolled over on her belly. Logan had changed the sheets and pillowcases while she had been in the bathroom—she hadn't realised that. The fresh linen felt smooth and cool.

Her eyelids fluttered to her cheeks. Yes, she'd go after him and find out exactly what he was up to. But she'd do it later. Later, not now...

When she awoke again, Logan was sitting beside the bed, reading a magazine. With some surprise, she recognised it as one of the stack she'd accumulated since she'd bought the house. It was an architectural digest; she'd picked it up because it headlined an article about restoring old New England homes like this one, even though she knew restoration was only a much too expensive pipe-dream.

He was reading it as if he was really interested. It was strange, but she'd never before seen him read anything other than a newspaper or a business report. Talia watched him for long minutes from under her lashes. He'd brought in the rocker from the living-room, and his feet were propped on an old hassock. He looked altogether different from how she'd ever seen him, she thought suddenly; he looked relaxed and comfortable and...

'Well. The lady awakens.' He smiled, closed the magazine, and tossed it aside. 'Feeling better?'

'Yes.' It was true, she did feel better. The light-headedness was gone, and she was hungry.

Logan's smile broadened. 'Good. Time for another tablet and then a trip to the bathroom, and then——'

'I can manage on my own,' she said quickly.

He paused, eyeing her narrowly. 'Are you certain?'

She wasn't. But the thought of having him bring the tablet to her lips, of tasting his skin and then having his arms close around her while he lifted her from the bed, was more than she could handle.

'I think so,' she said. Carefully, she sat up and swung her feet to the floor. The room swayed a little and she took a breath before taking first the tablet and then the glass he held out to her. She swallowed, then gave him a shaky smile. 'See? I'm not completely helpless.'

Logan's mouth twisted. 'Only a little,' he said, watching her, and then he smiled. 'OK. Let's see if you can make it to the bathroom on your own.'

She did. And she almost made it back. But halfway across the room, her legs buckled. Logan muttered an oath and caught her up in his arms.

'Enough of that nonsense,' he said. His arms tightened around her as he looked down into her face. 'From now on,' he growled, 'we'll do things my way.'

Talia linked her hands behind his neck. A tremor raced along her skin. His mouth was so close to hers—all she had to do was raise her head and she could put her lips to his. She swallowed and looked away from him. 'Could I—do you think it would be all right if I had some lunch?'

Logan grinned. 'I think it would be terrific. What would you like? Chicken soup? French toast? A cup of custard? Rice pudding, maybe. That's supposed to be good for invalids.'

Her eyes met his and she laughed softly. 'How are you going to manage any of that? Did a cook materialise in my kitchen overnight?'

He smiled back at her. 'Just put in your order and watch what happens.' They kept looking at each other. After a moment, Logan cleared his throat. 'Would you like to eat inside, by the fireplace? I can bundle you up and sit you on the couch.'

'Yes,' she said, while her foolish heart raced a million miles a minute, 'that sounds nice.'

He carried her into the living-room and settled her in a nest of pillows and blankets. She watched as he bent to the fire and added a fresh log, then crossed the room to the kitchen. She could just see him through the open doorway; there were pots on the stove and dishes on the centre counter. She sniffed, then sniffed again, for the first time noticing the lovely smells in the air—cinnamon and nutmeg, chicken and celery.

Her hands began to tremble and she clasped them together and put them in her lap. What was going on here? She knew why Logan had come—to try and talk her into accepting his job offer. But why had he stayed? The doctor had been here, he'd said. Surely the doctor could have made arrangements for her care. Logan could have seen to it . . .

'Luncheon is served, ma'am.' She looked up and he smiled as he set a tray down on the coffee-table. 'We have here some soup, some custard, and a dish of rice pudding.'

Talia laughed. 'Custard *and* rice pudding?'

'No good, huh?' He shrugged his shoulders as he squatted down on his haunches before her. 'Pick one, then. Your choice.'

'Where did all this stuff come from? I didn't——'

'No, you certainly didn't.' He waited as she took a spoonful of soup. 'How is it?'

'Good,' she said. 'Really good.'

He rose and sat down beside her. 'I made it.' His voice was smug.

Her eyes widened in disbelief. 'You? But how? I don't understand. You're not going to tell me you know how to cook?'

He laughed. 'No. I don't think I ever spent more than ten minutes in a kitchen, until this morning. We had a cook all the years I was growing up—Mrs Rothschild. And she didn't like anyone to intrude on her turf—especially small boys.' His smile faded a little. 'And my wife had no interest in cooking. In fact, it amazed me how quickly she was able to find and hire a woman who was a virtual Rothschild clone.'

'Then how . . . ?'

'The doctor told me the kinds of things he wanted you to eat. And you have three shelves of cookbooks in that kitchen.' He frowned. 'Of course, there wasn't a hell of a lot of food in the cupboards or the fridge. But the market up the road——'

Talia stared at him. 'You mean—you mean you shopped for all this stuff and then you cooked it?'

'Yeah.' He grinned. 'And from the looks of how quickly you're demolishing my efforts, I did a pretty good job.'

She was too stunned to do anything more than nod. He had done a fine job, she thought. The soup was good, the pudding delicious.

'Listen, I know you women tend to make food preparation sound like a cross between mysticism and quantum physics, but the simple truth is that anybody can manage—not creatively, maybe, but competently— if he or she can read and follow directions.' Logan smiled. 'True?'

She nodded. 'Yes,' she finally answered, 'true.'

True as far as it went, she thought. But what he'd left out of that easy equation was the most important part, and that was Logan Miller himself. This man, who'd shopped in the old-fashioned market up the road, who'd pored through her cookbooks and taken out her pots and pans, who'd painstakingly prepared the first meal he'd ever made in his life, was someone who had hardly ever gone into the kitchen of his apartment in Sao Paulo. For that matter, he'd never let her go into it, either, except to boil water for tea or coffee. What had possessed him to do all this?

'Logan.' Talia took a deep breath and put down her custard cup. 'I don't understand what's going on.'

Something flickered in his eyes. He rose to his feet, stuck his hands into the back pockets of his jeans, and looked away from her into the fire. 'Yes. You're right. Let's get to it.'

His voice had lost all tone. She felt a sudden chill. Shivering, she pulled the blankets more closely around her.

'Did I...?' She paused, then began again. 'I guess I passed out last evening.'

He nodded. 'Yes. I carried you to the couch, then called for a doctor.'

'And?'

'And he said you have a bug—a flu that's been making the rounds. Nothing serious.' He swung around and gave her an accusing stare. 'He also said you need to put some meat on your bones. I told him I'd never seen you this thin.'

A flush rose to her cheeks, but she forced her eyes to remain on his face. 'I wouldn't call it "thin",' she said stiffly. 'I'm slender, that's all. I always have been.'

'You're skin and bones,' Logan said flatly. 'You haven't been eating properly.' His mouth narrowed. 'I don't think you've been sleeping well, either. There are shadows under your eyes.'

She drew a deep breath. 'I appreciate your concern. And I'm grateful for everything you've done. But that doesn't give you the right to criticise me.'

A smile flickered across his face. 'Is that what you think I'm doing, Talia?'

The question, and the way he looked at her, sent a flutter along her skin. 'You—you still haven't told me how you found me,' she said.

He shrugged his shoulders. 'I told Diamond I had to get in touch with you. He gave me your address.'

Something seemed to die within her. So, she'd been right. Logan was here to try and convince her to work for him again. She'd known that all along, but hearing him admit it so readily was painful.

You're a fool, Talia. Did you really think that all this meant anything? He wants you to accept his job offer, that's all.

As for the shopping and the cooking, well, Logan wasn't the sort of man who could sit on his hands. He must have been bored to death, waiting for her to recover enough so that he could talk to her.

'Yes,' she said quietly. 'I spoke with John yesterday. He told me about your proposition.'

'He wouldn't tell me where you were, at first.' He took his hands from his pockets and placed them flat on the fireplace mantel. 'I told him he'd damned well better, or I'd cancel every last contract Diamond had signed with me.'

Talia closed her eyes. It wasn't hard to imagine him making such a threat. He always got what he wanted—he'd told her that at the start. OK, that took care of the preliminaries, she thought, while the room filled with silence. Now he would ask her to reconsider his job offer. He would tell her she was being stupid, that they worked well together.

Her breath caught. He might even say more than that. She'd seen what was in his eyes when he'd held her, she'd heard the thickness in his voice when he'd told her she was still beautiful. He was still attracted to her. Or perhaps he'd become attracted all over again. Whichever it was, the fire that had gone out—not for her, never for her—was rekindling for him. But she would never let it flame to life. Never.

She had lost him, she had lost his child, and the pain of both losses had almost paralysed her. She could not— she *would* not—go through such anguish ever again. If she did, she would surely die.

Slowly, carefully, Talia pushed the blankets aside and rose to her feet. 'Logan.' Her voice was low. He turned slowly, his eyes narrowing when he saw her standing there.

'What are you doing?' he demanded. 'You can't——'

'I want you to leave,' she said quietly. 'I'm grateful for everything you did—tending me, cooking for me, all of it—but...'

His lips drew back from his teeth. 'Did I ask for your gratitude?' A pulse leaped in her throat as he covered the distance between them in two strides. 'At least the scene's been rewritten,' he said angrily. 'Last time, you ran out. This time, you're sending me away.'

Talia swallowed drily. 'I didn't run out. I only did what—what we both knew had to be done. And now, I'm telling you——'

His voice cut across her. 'Why are you still wearing the amulet I bought you?'

Her hand went to the *figa*. 'That has nothing to do with——'

She gasped as he reached out and caught hold of her shoulders. 'Do you know what happened when I was undressing you last night?' His eyes searched hers. 'You looked at me, and you smiled and whispered my name; you put your palm against my lips, the way you used to when we made love.'

She drew in her breath, then expelled it sharply. 'That's a lie.'

'Is it?'

'Yes.' Talia touched her tongue to her lips. 'And even—even if it weren't,' she whispered, 'even if it weren't, you can't hold me responsible for something I did while I was delirious.'

'What can I hold you responsible for, then?' Logan's jaw set grimly. 'How about turning my life upside-down?'

'Me? *I* turned *your*——' She broke off, torn between the desire to laugh and to cry.

His fingers bit into her flesh. 'Why did you run away?'

'I told you, I didn't run.' She forced herself to look into his eyes. 'You wanted me to go, Logan. You as much as told me so.'

His mouth twisted in pain. 'Yes,' he said finally, 'I suppose I did. That's the reason I didn't go after you—I knew what we had had to end. I figured a clean break was the best kind.'

Talia nodded. 'And now you've changed your mind. You—you need me in Dallas. And you even think...' Her voice broke. 'You even think you might—you might want to pick up where we left off——'

'No!' The word was torn from his throat. Logan's eyes turned the colour of Arctic ice. 'No,' he repeated softly, 'not that. Never that.'

'I'm glad we agree,' she whispered. 'So you might as well leave, Logan. Because I'm not—I'm never...' To her horror, tears rose in her eyes. She felt them hang on her lashes, then begin to slide down her cheeks.

Logan made a choked sound, then groaned her name. 'Talia,' he said, and his arms went around her so tightly that she felt as if the breath were being forced from her lungs. 'Talia,' he whispered again, and he held her to him.

She sighed as she leaned into his comforting strength. It felt so good to be in his arms, so right, as if she had returned home after a long time in a cold and distant place. His hands stroked her, soothed her, while she inhaled his familiar scent, luxuriated in the steady beat of his heart beneath her ear. Talia knew she had to push him away, she had to tell him to leave and never return. But her life stretched ahead, the years lonely and barren. Surely she was entitled to these precious moments that would be all she would have of him after today.

Logan put her from him, then cupped her face and lifted it to his. The harsh pressure of his fingers branded her. 'Tell me something,' he said.

There was a silken thread in his voice that made her wary. 'What?'

'What are you doing here?'

She looked at him blankly. 'I don't understand.'

'When Diamond told me you'd quit your job, that you'd moved to a place like this, I thought he was crazy.' Logan's eyes were intent on hers. 'He said he couldn't make you change your mind, not even when he dangled a vice-presidency as bait.'

Talia's eyes slid from his. 'I—I wanted a change, that's all. Everybody's entitled to——'

'Why did you walk away from everything you'd worked for?'

'Because—because...' Her words faded away. Because I love you, she thought, because nothing I'd worked for meant anything without your love. She swallowed hard and raised her eyes to his. 'I—I know it's hard for you to understand,' she said carefully. 'But—but I realised—I realised I didn't really want the things I'd——'

Logan's fingers curved into her flesh. 'Weren't you ever going to tell me about our baby?' he said in a rough whisper.

The question staggered her. He knew! But how? How?

'Answer me, dammit!' His face twisted with pain. 'Didn't you think I had the right to know?'

Talia moistened her lips with the tip of her tongue. 'How—how did you find out?' she asked in a faint voice.

'The insurance company screwed up. They sent your medical forms to Sao Paulo a couple of days ago instead of to Diamond. Now answer me, dammit! Why didn't you send for me? Why didn't you tell me you were pregnant?'

She stared at him. 'Why would I have done that? I knew—I knew how you felt about—about having children. You didn't even want any when you were married; why would you——?'

Logan grimaced. 'What the hell are you talking about?'

Tears flooded her eyes again and she blinked them away. 'Children—children are just an impediment to a man like you.'

'God!' The single word was a cry of anguish rather than a curse. His face was pale, his eyes dark pools. 'We lived together for two months,' he said softly, 'but you never really knew a thing about me, did you?'

Talia swallowed hard. 'I knew enough,' she whispered brokenly. 'You have no room in your life for anything but the empire you've created. That's why your wife left you and I don't blame her. It must have been hell to love you but to always be second to your work, hell to love you but never lay claim to your heart.'

She was crying now, saying all the things she'd sworn never to tell him, but it didn't matter any more. Her pride was gone, lost in the pain of loving and losing him. Logan could think what he wanted of her, but he would finally hear the truth.

'I tried,' she sobbed. 'I tried so hard. I knew you didn't want me to intrude on your life—you didn't want to talk about anything that mattered, or spend a quiet evening home, or—or play cards or Scrabble or watch a crummy old movie on television...'

'Talia. Talia, my darling——'

'The worst of it is that I'd never wanted those things, either.' She rubbed her hand roughly across her eyes. 'Not until I met you. Not until I—until I...' Her voice broke. 'The only place you wanted me was in your bed, Logan, and after a while that broke my heart. I know you can't understand...'

He cursed softly, then pulled her to him. His mouth dropped to hers and he silenced her with a kiss so intense, so filled with sorrow and passion, that she moaned against his lips. But then she put her hands against his chest and pushed him away.

'What are you trying to prove?' she whispered. 'That I still want you? Yes. I do. I always will. But it's not nough. Don't you see? I—I wanted—I want so much more, I want ... I wanted——'

She broke off, sobbing, and Logan cradled her in his arms, gentling her with little kisses and whispers.

'Talia, Talia,' he murmured, 'how we've wronged each other.' Gently, he held her from him and his eyes fastened on hers. 'I know what you wanted. You wanted my love.' He smiled and stroked damp tendrils of hair from her cheeks, his thumbs easing lightly over her skin. 'And I wanted yours, darling. I wanted it more than I'd ever imagined.'

Talia's eyes widened. 'You—you wanted...?'

He nodded. 'Yes. But I was afraid to tell you. I thought it would scare you off. You'd made it clear that you wanted your career, not me. The only time you let me get close to you was when we made love. You were so giving in my arms, so loving...'

She looked at him. 'But—but that's how I felt about you, too. But you—you were so closed to me at other times... And we were never alone. You never wanted to be.'

'I was sure I'd say something that would give the game away.' He smiled crookedly. 'After a while, I couldn't keep up the charade, not even in bed. I wanted to tell you what you meant to me, not just show you. But I knew that, if I did, you'd run away. So I began to think up excuses to avoid making love to you.'

She was almost afraid to breathe. Was it true? Had he been hiding his feelings from her, just as she'd hid hers from him? 'Do you love me, Logan?' she whispered.

The look in his eyes made her heart swell with happiness.

'Yes,' he said, kissing her gently. 'I love you more than I ever thought a man could love a woman. I want us to make a home together, to have children...'

Time stilled while she looked deep into his eyes. There was a vulnerability in them she had never seen before.

'I—I can't believe it. You never wanted those things. That's why your wife left you—you had no time for her, you only had time for your business.'

Logan's mouth narrowed. 'Yes, that's the story she told, and I let her. But the truth is that I only buried myself in my work after our marriage collapsed.'

'Then—then why did your marriage fail?'

'Lenore married me because I gave her an entrée into a world she'd always coveted. She was fascinated with money, power, the social merry-go-round.' A muscle knotted in his jaw. 'I didn't know that at first, of course. When we were dating and I talked about the things I wanted—a real home, children—she always smiled and said yes, it all sounded wonderful.'

Talia's eyes swept over his face. 'But she didn't mean it?'

Logan shook his head. 'She had no interest in that kind of life. I suppose she thought she'd bring me around after we were married. She was a beautiful, clever woman, the kind who says one thing but means another.' He smiled. 'You impressed me by being the opposite.' He laughed when her brows rose enquiringly. 'Oh, you're beautiful,' he said, kissing the tip of her nose. 'Very beautiful. And bright. But you were honest about your ambitions. You knew what you wanted——'

'Until I met you,' she said, smiling. 'Do you remember when we met? You told me you liked the way I turned my emotions on and off. But it wasn't like that, Logan. What I felt for you terrified me; I knew, somehow, that my life was never going to be the same again. I'd planned it all so carefully, you see, and then suddenly, there you were, ruining everything.'

Logan laughed softly. 'You ruined everything for me, too, sweetheart. I'd sworn I'd never fall in love again— and then, there you were. My only safety lay in thinking you could control the situation.' He smiled a little. 'Because I sure as hell couldn't.'

Talia leaned back in his arms and looked up at him. 'And that day in Rio? We had such a lovely time until——'

'I think that was the day I realised I was falling in love with you. I was afraid to face the truth, so I tried to trivialise what I felt.' His hands cupped her shoulders. 'It didn't work, though,' he said. 'All that happened was that I fell deeper and deeper in love with you.' His eyes grew dark. 'I was so angry at you that last night in Sao Paulo, Talia. I knew it was foolish, but all the time I was away, I let myself play mind-games. I imagined you waiting for me at the apartment, eager for my return, as if I'd become the centre of your life, just as you'd become the centre of mine. But when I got there...'

'I was out. And when I finally showed up, I said I'd had more important things to do than wait for you.' She sighed. 'How terribly we've misunderstood each other, Logan, how...' She fell silent suddenly, and a terrible sadness wrenched at her heart. 'Logan,' she whispered, pressing her cheek to his chest. 'Can you forgive me for losing our baby?'

'There's nothing to forgive, darling. I'm just sorry you went through such an awful thing alone.'

Tears slid from beneath Talia's closed lashes. 'I—I thought about—about getting rid of it,' she said softly. 'But I would never have done it. I loved our baby. I...'

Logan tilted her face up and kissed her. It was a kiss filled with promise and tenderness, forgiveness and joy. When it ended, she was smiling.

'We'll have a houseful of babies,' he promised.

She sniffed back her tears, then laughed softly. 'And a Newfoundland dog.'

He smiled. 'Yes. And kittens and cats...'

She sighed happily. 'Is this a proposal?'

'It had better be. I'm sure as heck not going to move into a house filled with babies and cats and dogs unless you're there to take care of them with me.'

They smiled into each other's eyes and then Logan swung her into his arms.

'When do you have to be back at the office?' she whispered.

'Whenever I decide to get there. You'd be amazed how well things run without me.'

Talia shook her head as she linked her arms around his neck. 'Nothing runs smoothly without you.'

Logan grinned. 'So,' he said, sinking down before the fireplace with her still in his arms, 'what shall we do with the rest of the day, hmm? It's still snowing—for all I know, we're going to be snow-bound for a week.'

She sighed dramatically. 'Well, let's see. There's lots to eat. Chicken soup...'

'World-class chicken soup, if you please.'

She laughed. 'And the doctor's been here, so I have all the medication I need.'

Logan's eyes turned to emerald. 'Not all, sweetheart,' he whispered. He kissed her, and, when finally he raised his head, Talia's heart was racing as rapidly as his. 'I think I'm just going to have to administer my own therapy all through the day and into the night.'

'For the rest of our lives,' she said softly.

Logan smiled as he drew her down beside him. After a while, the only sounds in the room were the crackling of the logs on the hearth and the sound of the wind as it played softly through the eaves.

**THIS JULY, HARLEQUIN OFFERS YOU
THE PERFECT SUMMER READ!**

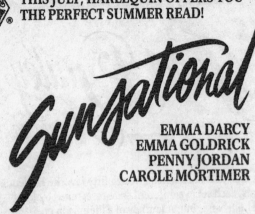

**EMMA DARCY
EMMA GOLDRICK
PENNY JORDAN
CAROLE MORTIMER**

From top authors of Harlequin Presents comes
HARLEQUIN SUNSATIONAL, a four-stories-in-one
book with 768 pages of romantic reading.

Written by such prolific Harlequin authors as Emma Darcy,
Emma Goldrick, Penny Jordan and Carole Mortimer,
HARLEQUIN SUNSATIONAL is the perfect summer
companion to take along to the beach, cottage, on your
dream destination or just for reading at home in the warm
sunshine!

Don't miss this unique reading opportunity.

Available wherever Harlequin books are sold.

Back by Popular Demand

Janet Dailey
Americana

A romantic tour of America through fifty favorite Harlequin
Presents, each set in a different state researched by Janet
and her husband, Bill. A journey of a lifetime in one
cherished collection.

In August, don't miss the exciting states featured in:

Title #13 — ILLINOIS
The Lyon's Share

#14 — INDIANA
The Indy Man

Available wherever
Harlequin books are sold.

JD-AUG

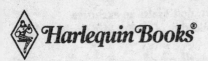**Harlequin Books®**

GREAT NEWS...

HARLEQUIN UNVEILS NEW SHIPPING PLANS

For the convenience of customers, Harlequin has announced that Harlequin romances will now be available in stores at these convenient times each month*:

Harlequin Presents, American Romance, Historical, Intrigue:

> May titles: April 10
> June titles: May 8
> July titles: June 5
> August titles: July 10

Harlequin Romance, Superromance, Temptation, Regency Romance:

> May titles: April 24
> June titles: May 22
> July titles: June 19
> August titles: July 24

We hope this new schedule is convenient for you.

With only two trips each month to your local bookseller, you'll never miss any of your favorite authors!

*Please note: There may be slight variations in on-sale dates in your area due to differences in shipping and handling.

*Applicable to U.S. only.

HDATES-RR

This August, don't miss an exclusive
two-in-one collection of earlier love stories

MAN
WITH A PAST

TRUE COLORS

by one of today's hottest
romance authors,

Jayne Ann Krentz

Now, two of Jayne Ann Krentz's most loved books are
available together in this special edition that new and
longtime fans will want to add to their bookshelves.

Let Jayne Ann Krentz capture your hearts with the love
stories, MAN WITH A PAST and TRUE COLORS.

And in October, watch for the second two-in-one
collection by Barbara Delinsky!

Available wherever Harlequin books are sold.

Harlequin Intrigue ®

Trust No One . . .

When you are outwitting a cunning killer, confronting dark secrets or unmasking a devious imposter, it's hard to know whom to trust. Strong arms reach out to embrace you—but are they a safe harbor . . . or a tiger's den?

When you're on the run, do you dare to fall in love?

For heart-stopping suspense and heart-stirring romance, read Harlequin Intrigue. Two new titles each month.

HARLEQUIN INTRIGUE—where you can expect the unexpected.

H A R L E Q U I N
American Romance®

From the Alaskan wilderness to sultry New Orleans...from
New England seashores to the rugged Rockies...American
Romance brings you the best of America. And with each trip,
you'll find the best in romance.

Each month, American Romance brings you the magic of
falling in love with that special American man. Whether an
untamed cowboy or a polished executive, he has that
sensuality, that special spark sure to capture your heart.

For stories of today, with women just like you and the men they
dream about, read American Romance. Four new titles
each month.

HARLEQUIN AMERICAN ROMANCE—the love stories you can believe in.

AMERICAN